WOMAN OF MYSTERY

While on a study holiday in Italy, researching the mysterious last paintings of Lorenzo Gagliardi, Jessica Matthews is advised to search out Noah Glassman, a visiting lecturer at the local university, for help. To her frustration, she finds him both abrasive and attractive. Events take a sinister turn when Noah's office is vandalised — and then a Gagliardi painting is damaged in a break-in at an exhibition. Who could have a motive for the crimes — and what secrets are waiting to be discovered within the ancient monastic foundations of the university?

Books by Ken Preston
in the Linford Romance Library:

FATE IN FREEFALL
DANGER IN PARIS

KEN PRESTON

WOMAN OF MYSTERY

Complete and Unabridged

LINFORD
Leicester

First published in Great Britain in 2017

First Linford Edition
published 2018

A catalogue record for this book is available
from the British Library.

ISBN 978–1–4448–3718–6

Published by
F. A. Thorpe (Publishing)
Anstey, Leicestershire

Set by Words & Graphics Ltd.
Anstey, Leicestershire
Printed and bound in Great Britain by
T. J. International Ltd., Padstow, Cornwall

This book is printed on acid-free paper

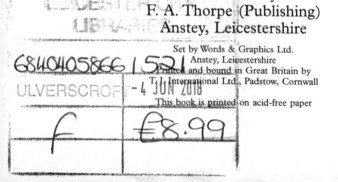

1

There hadn't been many times in Jessica Matthews' life that she had been left speechless, but now was definitely one of them. Realising she was standing there with her mouth hanging open, she snapped it shut and searched her mind for a pithy reply.

In the end, all she could come up with was a rather lame, 'Excuse me, but what did you just say?'

Noah Glassman, his back currently turned to her, swung around to face Jessica. He was sitting — no, not sitting; he was slouching — in a large swivel chair. The chair was obviously old and had seen better days. The leather upholstery was cracked and faded, and one of the arms was missing.

Noah Glassman was wearing a crumpled shirt open at the collar with a loosely knotted tie, creased trousers, and a pair of brown loafers that looked like they had gone out of fashion only a couple of years after Jessica had left nursery school. Adding to his general unkempt appearance, Noah's shaggy brown hair looked badly in need of a brush and his beard a trim. At least there didn't appear to be scraps of food sticking to it. That really would have been the last straw, and Jessica probably would have turned and fled.

Noah cleared his throat and ran a hand through his hair. 'I said, Mrs Matthews, that I'm not paid by the University of Trento to hold your hand while you indulge in some mid-life crisis of rediscovering your lost passion for art by trotting around Italy and writing up on the grand masters for some vacuous infotainment magazine in the UK.'

Once again, Jessica was left speechless. That wasn't what he had originally said, but rather an expanded, improved, more insulting version.

'Mid-life crisis?' she said. 'But I'm thirty-two!'

Noah waved a languid hand in dismissal. 'For all I care, you could be ninety-two. I'm not interested.'

Jessica thought he might turn his back on her once more and face his desk, but he didn't. He slouched in his old chair and stared up at her. Jessica was suddenly struck by the startlingly deep blue of his eyes. They were so clear and piercing that she had to look away. She fixed her attention to a spot just above his head, at the rows of art books crowding the shelves. Just like their owner, they were haphazard and dishevelled. Some of them looked in danger of falling apart, their bindings were so tattered, whilst others looked big enough to kill if they dropped from the shelves and landed on someone's head.

Or maybe knock some sense into Noah Glassman's head.

Jessica took a deep breath, gathering her thoughts.

'May I just check that you are Noah Glassman, visiting lecturer and artist in residence? The same Noah Glassman that Professor Bianchi advised me to come and see, who, he told me, would be very helpful and accommodating?'

'I'm afraid Mr Glassman has stepped out of the office for the foreseeable future.' Noah grinned. 'Sorry about that.'

'But wait, you're not . . . ?' Jessica faltered as she realised she was being made fun of.

'I know what you're thinking, Mrs Matthews. It must be rather a shock to find someone who doesn't immediately jump to his feet and trip over himself to give you everything you want. But look, I'm not all bad. We've just got off on the wrong foot, that's all.' Noah pulled open a drawer in his desk and took out a bottle of whisky and two glasses. He poured a generous slug into each glass and then held one out for Jessica. 'Have a drink. It'll remove the taste of lemon from your mouth.'

'Lemon?' Jessica said, frowning.

'Yeah, lemon,' Noah growled. 'From the expression on your face, you've obviously been sucking on one since you came into my office.'

Utterly horrified, Jessica stared at the glass of whisky held out for her. For the first time in her life, not only was she speechless, but she had no idea what to do next. Should she leave, slamming the door behind her? Should she find Professor Bianchi and report Noah Glassman for his rudeness? Perhaps she should just go back home to England and forget all about the research for her article.

'I have never been so insulted in all my life,' she said finally.

'I take it that's a no for the drink, then?' Noah replied. He downed the whisky himself and sat the glass on the desk.

Jessica watched in appalled fascination as he then downed the second glass of whisky. He reached out for the bottle, but then seemed to have second thoughts and left it where it was. He slouched back in his broken-down chair and gazed up at her.

'You're still here,' he mumbled.

'Do you often drink at work?' Jessica said.

'At work, at home. I've even been known to go and visit a bar and have a drink there sometimes. I find it helps the days go by a little smoother.'

'You're drunk, aren't you?' Jessica said, struggling to understand why the kindly professor would have sent her to this rude, arrogant man for advice on her research.

'Not quite,' Noah replied, 'but I'm getting there. Why don't you join me, Mrs Matthews? It's been a while since I got drunk in company.'

Jessica could stand it no longer. She had to say something, even though she had the distinct feeling she would regret it. 'For your information, Mr Glassman, I'm not Mrs Matthews but Miss.'

Noah held up his hands as though he was surrendering. 'I must apologise for my rudeness. I stand corrected.' His brow furrowed in thought. 'No, that's not right. I sit corrected.'

Was he making fun of her, or was that a genuine apology? Jessica decided to give him the benefit of the doubt for the moment. Although she had no idea why she should. Perhaps it was those piercing blue eyes. Or perhaps it was the fact that underneath that beard and all that hair, Noah Glassman was quite obviously very handsome. She had a hunch that if he were to have a shave, he would reveal a strong jawline, and she was certain now that he was a lot younger than she had first thought. It was the beard that made him look older.

'Mrs Matthews?' Noah said, breaking into her thoughts. 'Are we finished?'

Jessica was jolted back into the present, flushing slightly with embarrassment as she realised she had drifted off in thought. 'I suppose we have,' she said.

'No doubt I'll see you at the

exhibition tomorrow. I'm sure you'll find everything you need for your project there.'

'My . . . project?' Suddenly, anger rose in Jessica's chest. 'In case you hadn't noticed, I'm not some little girl at school doing a project for her homework! I happen to be writing an article for a reputable UK magazine about the recently discovered work of Lorenzo Gagliardi, and I was advised to come and see you as you are the foremost expert on Gagliardi's work. But all you've done since I stepped into your office is insult me!'

Noah looked hurt. 'That's not true.'

'Isn't it?'

'No. I offered you a drink.'

Jessica sighed in exasperation. 'Oh, you are such an infuriating man!'

Noah grinned. 'Yeah, but you like it.'

'That's what you think!' Jessica snapped, and turned on her heel to leave.

The idea had been to make a dramatic exit, maybe even slam the door behind her. But the door got caught on a bump in the floor beneath the carpet, and so she struggled to pull it open. When she finally managed to get outside, she didn't bother to close the door, and stalked off down the university corridor, her feet echoing off the wood-panelled walls.

Never before had she felt so infuriated, embarrassed and offended by someone.

And yet, at the same time, she had to admit there was something very attractive about Noah Glassman.

* * *

Noah stood up and walked over to the open door. He watched Jessica's retreating figure disappear around a corner at the end of the corridor, and then shut the door. He had been doing this a lot more recently — shutting his door on the rest of the university, shutting out the world.

Walking back over to his desk, he sat

down heavily in his chair. The chair creaked beneath his weight and he thought for a moment something might break and send him crashing to the floor. But it held and he was able to turn back to his desk and place his elbows on the top. Putting his head in his hands he let out a deep sigh.

Jessica Matthews had to be the prettiest young woman who had walked into his life in a long time. In fact, ever since . . . well, that was something he refused to dwell on. He knew he had to keep his thoughts fixed on the present, work on getting through each and every day.

Still, he couldn't stop thinking about Jessica. Her long wavy blond hair, slim build, and the way she was casually dressed in jeans and a T-shirt. She wasn't beautiful in a magazine-cover model sort of way. No, her beauty was much more natural and simple than that.

And he couldn't help but think now how he must have looked to her. Not exactly a work of art, was he?

Noah knew he had been rude and unpleasant with Jessica. It was the drinking that did that to him. And he had been drinking a lot more recently. Although he wouldn't have said he was drinking too much. On the contrary, he wasn't drinking enough. Not yet.

Noah picked up the bottle of whisky and unscrewed the cap. He was about to pour himself another generous serving when he paused, the bottle hovering over the empty glass.

A thought flashed into his mind of Jessica standing in front of him while he offered her a drink of whisky. All of a sudden he could see it from her point of view. How sad and silly he must have looked. He had thought he was being clever and witty, but no. Not when he put himself in her shoes.

Noah put the bottle down. Maybe he was drinking too much. He put the cap back on and then put the bottle back in the drawer. Ran his hand through his hair and then over his beard.

And maybe he could do with a haircut and a shave.

Noah blew out his cheeks in frustration and slammed his hand on the desk top.

'What do you think you're playing at, Noah Glassman?' he said to his empty office. 'One visit from a pretty young woman and she turns your head. Pull yourself together, man.'

Noah opened the desk drawer, took out the whisky bottle, and poured himself that generous serving after all.

★   ★   ★

Jessica walked through the university corridors, past the lecture halls and out of the arts faculty. She stepped outside into the glorious sunshine and found herself a bench to sit down on. The warmth of the sun, the blue sky and the snow-capped mountains visible in the distance immediately had a calming effect upon her nerves. The city of Trento in Northern Italy was situated in a dip between the mountains, and whichever direction you looked in you could always see the snow-tipped peaks. Jessica's landlady had said that some of the locals found being surrounded by mountains a little claustrophobic at times, but Jessica thought they were utterly beautiful and magnificent.

The city of Trento was also stunning, so very picturesque with its beautiful sun-bleached architecture. Jessica could almost see herself relocating here, and taking advantage of the clear light and beautiful scenery to learn to paint once more.

She sighed heavily. After her divorce from Harrison, she had fallen into a slump of despondency and listlessness, and this trip to Italy had been her parents' way of trying to lift her mood. They had paid for the trip, and her mother had even offered to come along for the two weeks. But Jessica had gently but firmly refused. She was grateful for the offer, but more than anything she wanted time away from her usual surroundings, and from all the familiar faces. Now that she was single again, it was perhaps a good time to rethink her life, and what she wanted out of it.

How she had ever imagined she and Harrison might be suitable marriage partners, Jessica could not fathom. Where she was artistic and passionate, he had been cool and analytical. Yes, he was an amazing surgeon and clinical teacher, but his life was so very ordered and structured that it sometimes drove Jessica mad. Some days (most days) she wanted to throw off the shackles of normal everyday life and do something fun and exciting and, yes, maybe even a tiny bit outrageous.

But not Harrison, her perfectly sensible husband.

She remembered that one time they were on holiday in the south of France. They had been on a secluded golden beach enjoying the sunshine when Jessica had suggested they take off all their clothes and run down to the water

14

where they could skinny-dip. There was hardly a soul within shouting distance, but Harrison had immediately balked at the idea, and he had raised all sorts of objections. Was nudity allowed on this beach? What if somebody saw them and called the police? Their clothes might be stolen while they were in the water. What would they do then? No, it was a silly idea.

Jessica sighed again. That was how Harrison had responded to most, if not all, of her ideas. And, although she couldn't see it at the time, over the five years that she was married to him, he had slowly but surely dampened her passionate spirit and her yearning for adventure.

If she hadn't found out about his affair with that anaesthetist and then divorced him, she might well have wound up just as boring as he was. Although he obviously had some passion in his life, to go out and have an affair, for crying out loud!

The betrayal still stung, but Jessica

knew she had been given a second chance. Now that she was free of her stifling marriage, it was her chance to reconnect with her younger self, the young woman who had studied Fine Art and loved to paint and draw. Who had wanted to travel the world, experience new cultures, and meet new people.

The only problem was her mother, who seemed intent on pairing Jessica up with another man as soon as possible. 'After all, your biological clock is ticking,' she loved to say. 'And if you wait much longer to have children, the alarm's going to go off, and then it will be too late!'

Thank you, darling Mother, Jessica thought.

Her mother only talked that way because she was concerned for her daughter, though. And if her mother could see her now, and knew what she was thinking about the rest of her life, she would be even more concerned. Her parents had paid for the trip with the intention that she relax and have some fun. Jessica was sure they were also secretly hoping she would meet some dishy Italian while she was here.

But Jessica had other plans. Before leaving the UK, she had been in touch with the editor at *Art World Magazine*. She had written a number of articles in her spare time for them in the years after she graduated, only stopping once she met Harrison and they started getting serious. She had been delighted that Malcolm Gladstone, the editor, was still there and remembered her.

'Jessica, where have you been?' he had said, his enthusiastic tones lifting her spirits even over the phone. Malcolm was one of those people who was always upbeat and encouraging, and very, very enthusiastic about anything and everything. It was impossible to be down in the dumps in his company.

It was Malcolm who had told her about the special exhibition of Lorenzo Gagliardi's work opening in Trento, at the Palazzo delle Albere. A series of paintings had been discovered by the early twentieth-century Italian artist, all of them portraits of the same beautiful young woman.

'And Jessica,' Malcolm had said, 'this young woman in the paintings is a complete mystery. No one has a clue who she might have been. You'll be our Sherlock Holmes, Jessica. Find out the identity of the young woman and why Gagliardi was so obsessed with her towards the end of his life, and you'll be a sensation in the art world. A sensation, my dear!'

Jessica smiled at the memory of the phone call. This was her 'holiday' then. Write an article on the late-period work of Lorenzo Gagliardi, and discover the identity of the mysterious young woman in his paintings.

Not much time for romance, then.

Jessica's mother would be horrified.

2

Jessica walked back through the city of Trento towards her lodgings. Despite her frustrating encounter with Noah earlier, she felt relaxed and, well, happy. This was an unusual feeling after all the drab years spent with boring Harrison. This was what she had needed for a long time: an adventure! Sunshine, a beautiful glamorous city, and a mystery to pursue. What could be better?

Jessica walked down a narrow alleyway in deep shadow. Ahead she could see the bright sunshine of the opening at the end of the alley, and the mountains in the distance beneath the deep blue of the sky.

When Jessica stepped out from the exit of the narrow street, she almost gasped with delight. Opening out before her was the Piazza Duomo, the vast open centre of the city. Thankful to be back in the warmth of the sunshine, Jessica walked through the city's square, admiring the cathedral dominating the opposite end. This was the Trento Cathedral, a stunning Romanesque-Gothic building built in 1212.

Dotted around the square were cafés and small independent art galleries and craft shops. Every Wednesday and Saturday, a huge market filled the square selling everything from food to clothes and crafts. Jessica made a mental note to come along to the next market.

Despite her sense of happiness, her encounter with Noah still niggled at the back of her mind. He obviously was going to be of no help with her research into the mystery woman in Lorenzo Gagliardi's paintings, which might make her job a little more difficult. But Jessica was never one to give up easily. She would go to the special exhibition tomorrow, even if it meant encountering Noah again. And she would do her research and write something up for Malcolm.

'Jessica!'

Was someone calling her name? A young couple walking past, arm in arm, turned and looked behind them at the sound of the voice calling out, and smiled. Jessica turned to see who was calling her, and had to smile too.

Professor Alessandro Bianchi was running across the square, waving his arms and shouting her name. Professor Bianchi was far from being the type of man who ran anywhere. Portly and with short legs, he was huffing and puffing, and his face was an alarming shade of red. Added to this were his tousled halo of grey curly hair bouncing up and down as he ran, and his shirt straining at his large belly, the buttons threatening to go flying at any second.

'Professor Bianchi, what on earth is wrong?' Jessica said as he approached.

The university professor had to wait while he caught his breath before he could explain anything. 'My dear,' he said finally, 'I've just spoken to Noah and found out how terribly he treated you. I must apologise, not only on behalf of the university, but personally as well.'

'Oh, you have nothing to apologise for,' Jessica said.

'On the contrary,' Professor Bianchi said. 'The University of Trento prides itself not only on its quality of teaching and research, but its hospitality to visiting students. Really, Mr Glassman was, how do you say it, well out of order in the way he treated you.'

Jessica giggled.

'Did I say something funny? My English, it is not quite what it should be.'

'Oh no, Professor, your English is perfect,' Jessica said. 'But you should maybe just use the phrase 'out of order' from now on. 'Well out of order' is more a sort of street slang used by a certain type of teenager.'

'Ah, I see,' the professor said, and with a twinkle in his eye added, 'It's nice to know that even at my age I can still get down with the kids!'

Jessica laughed again.

'And please, you must stop calling me Professor. You make me feel even older than I actually am. It's Alessandro, my dear.'

'But really, you had no need to chase after me through the city centre,' Jessica said. 'Why didn't you call me?'

Alessandro waved his hand in dismissal. 'Pah, so impersonal. That is not the Italian way. I can only apologise to you face to face.'

Jessica opened her mouth to object, to repeat that no apology had been necessary from the professor, but he silenced her with another wave of his hand.

'You must come back to the university now, and I will buy you a drink and we can talk about Lorenzo Gagliardi.'

'Oh no, Prof — Alessandro, that's really not necessary.'

'Nonsense; of course it is. And besides, it will be my pleasure. It is not often that I have the opportunity to escort a beautiful young woman through the city. We shall turn a few heads, yes? And then the news will travel back to Signora Bianchi, and she will be jealous and she will cook my favourite meal for me tonight to woo me back into her arms.' And with that, he placed his arm through hers and they started walking back through the piazza.

'You must try not to judge Noah too harshly,' Alessandro said as they walked. 'There has been much sadness in his life, and this is why on some days he turns to the drink.'

'Oh, I didn't realise,' Jessica said.

The older man nodded. 'It happened some years ago — a terrible car accident in which his fiancée died. He has never fully got over the loss, and on some days the blackness descends upon him, and that is when he turns to the bottle. I should let him go, but he is a dear friend of mine, and usually the drink never affects his ability to do his job. Today really was an exception.'

A pang of sadness cut through Jessica's heart. He had treated her badly, but now her anger was tempered with sympathy for him. 'Oh, that's terrible,' she said.

'Yes, yes,' Alessandro replied. 'And in all these years since, he has remained single. It seems he is wedded to his art now, and his art alone.'

That's no way for anyone to live, Jessica thought. *No way at all.*

★ ★ ★

Back at the university, the professor took Jessica straight to the café, and the first thing she saw was Noah sitting at a table nursing a large black coffee.

'Oh no, did you know he was going to be here?' Jessica said.

Alessandro patted her arm and replied, 'I told him to meet us. It is important that he apologise to you himself'

'But, Professor Bianchi — '

'Please, my dear, it is Alessandro.'

'But I'll be so embarrassed, and so will he. Do you really think this is necessary?'

'I do,' the Professor replied in a kindly tone. 'For too long I have left him alone because he is my friend, and also because he is a brilliant artist and lecturer. But the university's governing body have begun to take notice of his attitude, and I fear that unless he takes action and smartens himself up, there may well be serious consequences.'

'Do you think they might sack him?'

Alessandro shrugged. 'Not right away, but it can only be a matter of time before he insults somebody enough that they take out a complaint against him.'

'But I'm not going to take out a complaint against him!'

The professor patted her arm. 'No, my dear, I know. But this is my way of driving home the point that his actions have consequences. For too long I have let him dwell on the past. Now he needs to turn his face to the future, and take life once more by the scruff of the neck!'

'Well, if you think so . . . '

'I do. Come now, go and take a seat with him while I buy us all a drink of coffee.'

Jessica nodded, still unsure that she actually thought this was a good idea, and slowly made her way towards Noah's table. She was surprised when Noah stood up as she approached, and pulled out a chair for her.

'Miss Matthews, I believe I owe you an apology,' he said rather stiffly.

'Well, you were rather rude to me, even if you did offer me a whisky,' Jessica said, unable to keep the hint of a smile off her face.

'Ouch,' Noah said, and smiled. 'But I suppose I deserved that. Please, sit down.'

Noah waited until Jessica was seated before sitting down too. She could hardly believe her eyes and ears. The rude, arrogant man of just half an hour ago had seemingly disappeared. What on earth had Professor Bianchi said to him to bring about such a change?

'Can we start again?' Noah said. He held out his hand. 'I'm Noah Glassman, visiting lecturer and artist in residence, although I have been here so long now that I'm surprised no one has thought to change my title to permanent lecturer and artist nobody can get rid of.'

Jessica took his hand and shook it. 'And I'm Jessica Matthews, of indeterminate age and going through a mid-life crisis whilst writing up an article for a vacuous infotainment magazine.' Jessica felt bad about the dig as soon as the words had left her mouth.

'Ouch again,' Noah said, only this time he didn't smile.

'I'm sorry, that was unkind of me.'

Noah ran his hand through his unkempt hair. Although it most definitely needed a trim, Jessica decided that the hair and the beard lent a certain roguish element to his appearance. And those clear blue eyes of his pierced her insides every time he looked at her. Even in his rather dishevelled state, Jessica would have thought he'd still have girls chasing after him.

And maybe he did. Apart from what Alessandro had told her on the way over, Jessica knew very little about Noah Glassman. Maybe he was still in a deep pit of sadness and grief over the loss of his fiancée, and maybe he was wedded to his art, but that didn't mean he had never had a relationship with another woman in the years since.

Alessandro interrupted the uncomfortable silence that had grown between Jessica and Noah by arriving at their table with three coffees on a tray.

Jessica looked in surprise at her own coffee, a shot of espresso in a mug with a jug of steaming hot water next to it.

'You dilute the espresso with the hot water to your preferred strength,' Noah said. 'This is how they serve coffee in Italy.'

'Oh, I see,' Jessica replied. She poured some of the hot water into her coffee and added a dash of milk.

'Now, how are we all getting on?' Alessandro asked, beaming at her and Noah in turn.

'Don't worry, Alessandro, I've made my apologies,' Noah said. 'And I do believe they may have been accepted?' He raised his eyebrows and looked at Jessica.

'Yes, yes, of course,' she said, flustered once more by those piercingly blue eyes. She placed her mug back in its saucer, and it rattled slightly. *What's wrong with me? I need to get a grip!*

'Oh that is very good,' Alessandro said. 'I do hope we can all be friends now.'

Jessica, desperate to change the subject, said, 'This part of the university looks much older than the rest.'

'But don't you know the history of the university building?' Alessandro said, his bushy eyebrows raised in comical astonishment.

'I'm sorry, but no,' she replied, and quickly took a drink of her coffee to hide her smile of amusement.

Alessandro indicated the stone arches sweeping up to the roof, and the glass wall separating the café from what looked like the interior of a church or a cathedral.

'This was part of the Abbey of San Vigilio, perhaps the oldest building in Trento, and certainly older than our magnificent cathedral,' the professor said.

'And now it's part of the university?' Jessica asked.

'Building the university on as a kind of extension helped ensure the abbey ruins would be preserved for future generations to enjoy,' Noah said. 'Visitors and tourists can still enjoy the abbey, but the students get to use it too. I hold several art classes in there over the course of an academic year, the student choral society sing in there, and I believe the history department has a semester covering the history of the abbey and the legends associated with it.'

'And one of those legends will be of great interest to you,' Alessandro said.

'Oh, really?' Jessica replied, intrigued.

'Yes indeed. The legend of Julian the Hospitaller. I'm surprised you haven't — '

'*Professore! Professore!*'

Everyone turned at the sound of the voice calling for Professor Alessandro. A young student was dashing through the café between the tables. Looking at his youthful face, Jessica was reminded of Noah's insult; and suddenly she did feel, if not middle-aged, far too old to be here amongst all these students.

'What on earth is wrong?' Professor Alessandro said.

'*Professore, l'unione degli studenti sono in possesso di un incontro — !*'

'English, please, Giovanni, in front of our guest,' Professor Bianchi said.

The young man took a deep breath. 'The student union are refusing to go to lectures today, and are holding a protest outside the university. No one can get in or out!'

Alessandro sighed and quickly gulped down his coffee. 'Please excuse me,' he said. 'Jessica, it was my pleasure to walk with you through our city centre, and I hope we have the opportunity to meet again before you leave.' He turned to face Noah. 'Remember what I said, won't you, Noah?'

Jessica watched as the professor bustled away with the young student, talking at a rate of knots in Italian. 'What was all that about?' she asked.

'Oh, there's some protest going on about a debate that is happening this evening at the university,' Noah said.

Jessica turned back to face him and gazed at him for a moment. That wasn't what she had meant. She had wondered what the professor had said to Noah that he didn't want him to forget. But now she suddenly felt it would be rude of her to ask. Instead, she said, 'What debate?'

'I haven't been following it, to be

honest. Something about the boundaries between Italy and Austria being moved. Did you know the Trentino region of Italy was once part of Austria?'

Jessica sipped her coffee and shook her head.

'And now there's this right-wing movement that are demanding the borders be shifted again to take Trentino back. Anyway, if you've finished your coffee, how about we go into the abbey while I explain about the legend of Julian, and what the connection is to your proj — sorry, I mean research.'

Jessica smiled inwardly. Noah Glassman was trying his best, she had to admit. Whatever it was that Professor Bianchi had said to him, it was working.

★   ★   ★

The inside of the abbey building was cool and quiet. The glass wall between the abbey ruin and the university café was surprisingly good at cutting out the noise of clinking crockery and the chatter of people. A person could even come here to pray or meditate. Facing the chancel meant turning away from the sight of the café through the glass wall and door. Calling it a ruin was no longer appropriate, even though that was what everyone still did. The walls and ceiling had been repaired sympathetically for the period it was built in so that it could be used again. But there was only really half an abbey, ending where the modern university building met the ancient place of worship.

'So,' Jessica said, 'tell me about the legend of Julian.'

Noah was looking up at the vaulted ceiling as he started to talk, and so Jessica was able to observe him without any self-consciousness. Yes, underneath all that hair he was definitely a very handsome man.

'The legend says that on the night Julian was born, his father, a man of noble blood, saw three witches hex the baby boy so that he would one day murder his parents. The father returned to his wife to tell her what he had seen, but she persuaded him to let the boy live, she loved him so much. The years passed and he grew into a fine young man, and everyone who saw him remarked how beautiful he was. But all the while his parents kept this terrible secret. Finally Julian's mother told her son about the curse laid upon him, and he vowed to leave and go as far away as possible, so that he would never murder his parents, who he loved very much.'

Noah paused in his story and lowered his head to look at Jessica. Flustered, Jessica looked away, hoping that Noah hadn't noticed the sudden flush of heat to her cheeks. Her thoughts had strayed from the story, and she realised she had been imagining giving Noah a shave and trimming his hair. Many years ago she had had ambitions to become a hairdresser and had taught herself to cut hair. She would often cut her dad's hair, her friends', and Harrison's too, although she never did try for a job at a hairdresser's.

What's wrong with you? she thought. *You're acting like a giddy teenage girl.*

'Am I boring you?' Noah said.

'No, not at all,' Jessica replied.

'Oh, it's just that your mind seemed elsewhere.'

Was he teasing her? Had he realised what she was thinking? That was a silly idea; of course he hadn't. 'No, please carry on with the story,' she said.

'Well, as long as you're not bored,' Noah said, the hint of a smile playing across his face. 'Having promised his mother he would never do such a terrible thing, Julian left and travelled many miles until he met a woman he fell in love with. She was said to be a wealthy widow, and she and Julian were very happy together.' He paused.

'That's not much of a story.'

'Don't you like happy endings?'

'Well, yes, of course; but it's just not

the sort of thing you expect in a story like this.'

'Then you'll be pleased to know that there's more to come, I was just pausing to gather my thoughts when you interrupted me.'

Jessica glanced at Noah. Was he angry with her? No, that faint smile was still there.

'Twenty years passed, and Julian's parents decided to go looking for their son. They visited a church and stopped to pray at the altar. When they left the church, they encountered a woman sitting outside, and asked if there was anywhere nearby they could stay. The woman invited them into her own home — '

'Wait a minute, was this Julian's wife?' Jessica asked.

'How did you guess?' Noah said, raising an eyebrow.

'I had a feeling,' Jessica replied. 'It's a bit of a coincidence, the parents finding Julian's wife just happening to be sitting outside the first church they visit, don't you think?'

'How do you know this is the first church they visited?'

'You didn't mention any other churches.'

'Well, pardon me, but I don't happen to have an itemised list of all the churches they visited during their travels to find their missing son.'

'That's a shame,' Jessica said, unable to hide her amusement anymore.

'You're teasing me, aren't you?'

'I might be,' Jessica said, and thought to herself, *I think actually I might be flirting with you.* 'It's still a coincidence, though, isn't it?'

'It's a legend, a tale that's been passed down the centuries. What were you expecting? A signed, witnessed, fact-checked document of authenticity to go with the story?'

Jessica couldn't decide how serious Noah was. Was he teasing her back now, or was he genuinely annoyed? She thought, *Maybe it's best if I just stop with all the silly questions.*

'All right, I'm sorry,' she said. 'Could you tell me the rest, please?'

'Are you sure?'

'I'm sure.'

'Where was I?'

'Julian's parents had just found his wife sitting outside the church they'd been praying at.'

'Oh yes, that big coincidence. What a stroke of good fortune that was for them, although neither the parents nor the wife knew who each other was. And I shouldn't say it was a stroke of good fortune, considering how things turned out in the end.'

'Don't spoil it for me.'

'I'm sorry?'

'The ending to the story. You almost gave it away.'

Noah sighed heavily.

Jessica thought, *Just shut up and let him tell the story!*

'So Julian's wife took the parents back to her house, where she offered them her bed for the evening, telling them that her husband Julian was out hunting for the night. The parents were overjoyed when they realised they had found their son, as was the wife when they told her who they were.' He stopped and gazed at Jessica.

'Is everything all right?' she asked.

'Absolutely. Everything's fine.'

'Is that the end of the story?'

'Oh no, there's more to come.'

'But why have you stopped telling it?'

'I was just waiting for you to interrupt again, explain how there must have been hundreds of Julians around at the time, and about how easily the woman believed the parents when they told her that her husband was their son.'

Noah grinned, and Jessica realised he *was* teasing her now.

'Just get on with the story, will you?' she said, and punched him lightly on the arm.

Noah, making a big show of rubbing at his arm, said, 'While he was still out hunting, the enemy found him and told him that his wife had taken another

41

man into her bed, and that they were still there now, embracing.'

'Who was the enemy?'

'No one knows, but I suspect that's simply a term for the devil. Filled with sadness and rage, Julian hurried back to his house to find two figures asleep in his bed. He took his sword and slew them where they lay.'

'Oh no.'

'When he went back outside, he found his wife, who told him that his parents were resting in their bed. Julian fell into a rage, cursing the day he had been born. He returned to the forest and found the enemy who had lied to him, and drew his sword and attempted to slay him. But when his sword pierced the enemy's side, the enemy disappeared in a puff of smoke and sulphur. From that point on, Julian vowed to serve Christ, and he built hospitals and houses for the poor, and gave away much of his wealth of gold and silver.'

'What a sad story,' Jessica said.

'If a little thin on plausibility.'

'You're not going to let me forget that, are you?'

Noah shrugged. 'Probably not, no.'

'But what does all this have to do with Lorenzo Gagliardi and his paintings of the mysterious young woman?'

'I'm glad you asked. Come with me.'

Noah led her through the abbey ruin and down a narrow flight of stone stairs. Jessica noticed the modern additions to the ancient abbey, such as the handrail and the repaired edges to the steps.

Down at the bottom was a narrow crypt, the walls illuminated by two spotlights pointing up from the floor. At the end of the crypt were a pair of bronze two-foot-high statuettes of a man, set into an alcove. Features such as eyes and a moustache had been rather crudely painted onto the faces. Both men were wearing a gold chest-piece and holding a sword.

Noah held out his hand towards the statuettes. 'Jessica, meet Julian the Hospitaller, patron saint of hunters.'

'Which one's Julian?'

'They both are.'

'Oh. I thought maybe one was Julian and the other one was his twin.'

Noah sighed — rather dramatically, Jessica thought. 'No, we just happen to have two statues of Julian down here.'

'Is he buried here?'

'No — not as far as we know, anyway. But as far as the legend goes, Julian's sword, having struck the enemy, became imbued with a dark supernatural power, transferred from the devil into the blade. Because it was now too powerful and dangerous to be handled by any man, Julian entrusted it to the abbey for safeguarding by the monks.'

'But I still don't see what this has got to do with Lorenzo Gagliardi,' Jessica said.

'Before he devoted his life to the arts and specifically painting, Lorenzo was a man of faith, a monk at this very abbey.'

'Oh!' Jessica gasped. 'I hadn't realised.'

Noah smiled. 'No, I suspected not.'

Jessica suddenly realised how close they were standing. The crypt was tiny, and they had unconsciously moved toward to each other. In the silence, Jessica could hear Noah's soft breathing, and she could smell the freshness of his clothes. Despite what Professor Bianchi had said about Noah letting himself go, it seemed he hadn't let himself go too far. But then Jessica caught a hint of whisky on Noah's breath, and she remembered the scene in his office, and the drinking. It seemed Noah Glassman was a man of contradictions.

'Are you all right?' he asked.

Jessica suddenly realised she felt flushed and hot. When they had first stepped into the crypt, it had been cool. What was heating her up so much? Was it Noah's body, standing so close to hers? She had a sudden, almost irresistible urge to stand even closer, so that their bodies were touching. Where had that come from? And what would

Noah's reaction be if she did? They had only just met!

'I think I should get you upstairs,' Noah said. 'You look in need of some fresh air.'

And the moment was broken and Jessica stepped away from Noah, and said, 'Yes, yes, I think you're right.'

They climbed the steps back up to the abbey, and as they emerged from underground, Jessica could see the busy café on the other side of the glass wall.

And it seemed to her like she had stepped from one world into another.

3

The following day, Jessica awoke to the sound of birdsong, and sunlight streaming through her bedroom window. She stretched and sighed with contentment. From downstairs came the sounds of Stefania in the kitchen. Stefania and her husband rented out the spare bedroom in their house to visitors to Trento, and they had a thirteen-year-old daughter and seven-year-old boy. They were such a lovely family, and Jessica caught herself imagining what it might be like to simply come and live with them.

Don't be silly! she thought. *You're not moving out here, you're on a two-week holiday and assignment. You need to get your act together and get on with your research for this article.*

Jessica had a shower and then put on a simple summer dress. Just the sort of thing that Harrison would have disapproved of. Oh, he wouldn't have said anything, but Jessica would have known from the look on his face.

She loosely tied her hair back off her face and quickly moisturised, then twisted around and looked at the back of her neck in the mirror. *Must remember to put sun cream on today before I go out*, she thought. She hadn't caught the sun too much yet, but she risked sunburn today if she was out too long without protection.

Downstairs in the kitchen, Stefania was preparing coffee whilst her two children sat at the table eating their breakfast. 'Good morning!' she said, giving Jessica a broad smile.

Before Jessica could answer, Tomasso had leaped to his feet and, holding his fists in the air like a boxer, said, 'Hey you! You wanna fight?'

Jessica immediately fell into a crouch, holding her own fists out and said back to Tomasso, 'Hey you! You wanna fight?'

This sentence was the only English Tomasso knew, having seen it on a children's TV show, and he repeated it every time he saw Jessica. The ritual completed, the little boy sat down and continued with his breakfast.

'Good morning, Caterina,' Jessica said to the girl. 'Good morning, Stefania.'

'There are rolls on the table and butter and jam, or there is cereal for you,' Stefania said, beaming.

'Thank you,' Jessica said, sitting down opposite Tomasso's sister. 'And what are you doing today, Caterina?'

The girl pulled a face and said, 'School.'

Jessica laughed. 'I felt exactly the same way about school when I was your age. But now I'm older, I realise what a fantastic opportunity I had to learn so much. What lessons have you got today?'

Caterina pulled another face. 'We've got history first period, and it's boring.'

'Caterina!' Stefania said. 'You

mustn't talk in that way.'

Jessica leaned in closer to Caterina and lowered her voice a little. 'You know what? I didn't much like history when I was at school, but now? Now I find myself in your beautiful country, researching some your history, and I love it!'

'What are you doing today, Jessica?' Stefania asked.

She sat up straight again. 'I'm heading on over to the fortress for the first day of the Lorenzo Gagliardi exhibition.'

'Oh yes,' Stefania said, smiling. 'This famous Italian artist I have never heard of before.'

'You might be hearing a lot more of him soon,' Jessica said, picking up a roll and buttering it. 'These paintings of his that are on exhibition are a recent find, and are causing a small sensation in the arts world.'

Stefania sat down with two cups of coffee and handed one to Jessica.

'And why is that?' Stefania said.

'Gagliardi was never regarded in any sort of high esteem during his lifetime, or even after, to be honest,' Jessica said. 'Where his contemporaries, such as Picasso and Georges Braque, were changing the face of modern art with their stylistic approach to painting, Gagliardi was stuck in the Renaissance period.'

Stefania laughed and swept her hand over the top of her head. 'You've already lost me!'

Jessica smiled. 'You've heard of the style of painting called cubism, yes?'

Stefania nodded.

'Picasso and Braque pioneered this new form of art by painting their subjects as fragments of different views. Say if I was painting a portrait of you, Stefania — I'd paint you from all different angles so that the painting was fragmented and almost divided up into cubes.'

Caterina was also listening intently to Jessica talk. Only Tomasso was continuing to eat breakfast.

'But Gagliardi remained stuck in a style of painting known as Renaissance art that had emerged in Italy during the fourteen hundreds. He was considered old-fashioned, continuing to paint portraits and landscapes in a faithfully representational way. Technically he was an excellent painter, but stylistically he was very dull indeed.'

'But what is different about these paintings of his that were discovered so recently?' Stefania said.

'During the Second World War, during the German occupation of Italy, Gagliardi was imprisoned in the Palazzo delle Albere. No one really knows why, and after the war he became somewhat of a recluse until his death in nineteen fifty-six. It was always assumed that after his release from captivity, he never painted again. But it turns out that he *was* painting, and that stylistically he had freed himself from the constraints that previously held him back.'

Jessica looked at Caterina. The young

girl had been obviously interested at the beginning of Jessica's story, but now she was starting to look bored. Jessica lowered her voice again to a conspiratorial whisper, and said, 'But do you know what the most mysterious thing about all this is?'

Caterina shook her head.

'All of the paintings that Gagliardi produced during this period when he hid himself away were portraits of the same beautiful young woman, done over and over again. Gagliardi was obsessed with her.'

'But who was she?' Caterina asked, eyes wide.

'No one knows,' Jessica replied. 'And that's what I've come here to find out.'

'I bet she was his girlfriend,' Caterina said.

'Maybe,' Jessica replied, smiling. 'But the only way to find out is to look back into the history of his life. What do you think now? Do you still think history is boring?'

Caterina pulled a face again. 'That's

not boring, but the history lessons we have at school are.'

'Caterina!' Stefania scolded, laughing.

'Well, maybe you can help me out with my history lesson, and help me solve the mystery of the woman in the paintings,' Jessica said.

Caterina nodded enthusiastically. 'Can I help Jessica?' she asked her mother.

Smiling, Stefania said, 'Yes, of course. But first, breakfast and then school!'

★ ★ ★

Jessica took her time walking through Trento, admiring the architecture and the ever-present views of the snow-tipped mountains visible in the distance above the rooftops. She still couldn't get over how strange it was to be seeing snow, even if in the distance, whilst basking in the warmth of summer sunshine. The streets were busy with cars and buses as the city's residents bustled about their daily routines.

The Palazzo delle Albere was a Renaissance villa-fortress. Its name meant 'Palace of the Trees', as it had once been surrounded by rows of poplars. After a fire in 1796 almost destroyed it, the fortress went into a serious decline and was taken over by the Germans during the Second World War. But since then, it had been turned into a tourist attraction and was regularly used by the Trento Museum of Modern and Contemporary Art as a gallery space.

Jessica walked up the long gravel path and over the moat towards the massive square fortress. Her breath was almost taken away by the sight of the mountain behind the fortress, so imposing it almost seemed as though it would fall down upon her and swallow her up. At the fortress entrance, she showed her pass to the man on the door. Today, courtesy of Professor Bianchi, Jessica was a VIP guest for the opening of the

Gagliardi exhibition.

Although Jessica would have loved to explore the fortress, she hurried on to the main exhibition area. As she stepped through the large doorway, her heart did a quick double beat at the sight of Noah. His hair was still in need of a brush, and his beard in need of a trim, but he looked somehow smarter than yesterday.

And just as handsome. Jessica remembered standing close to him in the abbey's crypt, how she could almost feel the heat coming off him, and her breath caught a little at the memory of it.

Noah noticed her and she quickly glanced away, suddenly feeling her cheeks grow warm. She hadn't been aware that she had been staring at him. How long had she been doing that for?

Noah began heading towards her. The gallery space was busy, with men in suits and women in simple but formal dresses. Jessica was painfully aware of her summer dress and how out of place she looked. Even Noah looked smarter than she did!

As he approached her, he picked up two flutes of white wine from a linen-covered table. Jessica hadn't realised the opening of the Gagliardi exhibition was going to be such a grand event. Now she felt even more out of place, like the little schoolgirl doing her project that Noah had accused her of being yesterday. The truth of Noah's accusation stung Jessica and her cheeks heated up even more. Surely her face was glowing bright red by now. If it was night-time, the gallery could save a fortune on lighting by employing her to stand in the middle of the room and illuminate the space.

Noah had almost reached Jessica, a smile and a greeting forming on his lips, when he was interrupted by a woman who stepped in front of him.

'Noah Glassman!' she said, and took one of the wine glasses from his hand.

That was meant for me! Jessica thought. She waited for Noah to take the wine back from the woman, to make his excuses and continue to make his way to her.

'Cora, how are you?' he said, and they leaned in to each other and kissed on the cheeks.

No! Jessica thought, and for a moment she was afraid she had spoken the word out loud. *You weren't coming over to speak to her, you were coming to talk to me. Tell her!*

Noah turned slightly so that he was now facing away from Jessica as he continued to talk to the woman called Cora. And then some guests wandered between Jessica and Noah and she lost sight of him.

Jessica took a deep breath in an attempt to compose herself. *You're being silly and dramatic,* she told herself. *After all, it was only yesterday that he was insulting you and making fun of you.*

But then he did apologise, a more reasonable and calming voice told herself.

Yes, but only because Professor Bianchi told him to!

Jessica shook her head and walked away. This was silly, standing by herself in the middle of a crowded gallery arguing with herself over a man she had only met yesterday and who she didn't even like. Except, she sort of did like him, didn't she?

Jessica took a champagne flute of sparkling wine from a table and took a sip. It was lovely and clear and refreshing. But it did nothing to lighten her mood. *Maybe I should just leave,* she thought. *Get away from all these people, away from Noah and that woman.*

There was something about her that Jessica instinctively disliked, and it wasn't just the fact that she had interrupted Noah when he was obviously on his way to talk to Jessica. The way that she had presumed she could just take the wine from him when it must have been clear to her that it was meant for somebody else.

And Jessica found her appearance unsettling. She was tall, her straight dark hair cut into a bob. High-heeled boots accentuated her height, and her long legs looked stunning in straight slim-fit trousers and a close-fitting shirt. All in black, of course.

No, Jessica had decided, she didn't like that woman at all. It wasn't really in Jessica's nature to take an instant dislike to someone. But this time was different.

Rather than obey her instincts and leave, she decided to stay and do what she had originally come to Italy for: take a good look at Lorenzo Gagliardi's portraits and continue her investigation into the mystery woman in the paintings.

Wandering up and down the gallery space, trying to keep her mind on her assignment, Jessica was struck by how each painting of the unknown sitter was executed in such a different style to Gagliardi's previous work. Whereas before his work had always been very formal and precise, these newly discovered paintings were flamboyant and energetic. Some of them were almost abstract in the way in which the paint had been layered on, over and over in a seemingly frenzied outpouring of energy.

And yet the mysterious young woman always shone through the painting. She had long blond hair and a fiercely intensive gaze. Her stance was almost aggressive; and indeed, her right hand was clenched in a fist at her side.

'I'm not sure about you, but I don't think I would have actually wanted to meet her.'

'Oh!' Jessica gasped and turned.

Noah was standing by her side, two champagne flutes of sparkling wine in his hands. 'Here,' he said, handing her one. 'I'm sorry I got intercepted last time. Cora really does have a way of getting what she wants, and forget about everybody else.'

'Yes, I had that feeling about her,'

Jessica replied, holding a glass in each hand.

Noah took her empty glass and placed it on a nearby table.

'So, what do you think of Gagliardi's late-period work?' he asked.

'It's . . . so very different from anything else he painted.'

'Indeed it is. In fact, it's so dramatically different that at first there was tremendous doubt that these had anything to do with Gagliardi at all.'

'Then how do you know he did paint them?' Jessica asked, and took a sip of her wine.

'We've had them analysed by several experts in early twentieth-century art, and a Gagliardi specialist in particular. And we had a tiny sample taken from one of the paintings and had it carbon dated. All the evidence points to these paintings being the work of Lorenzo Gagliardi, despite the marked contrast in style from his previous work.'

'So there are two mysteries then, aren't there?' Jessica said. 'Not only do we not know the identity of the woman in the paintings, but neither do we know why Gagliardi suddenly switched from the Renaissance style of painting to this new, more original way of working.'

'That's right,' Noah said. 'Looks like you've got your work cut out for you, doesn't it?'

Jessica looked at him quizzically. 'What do you mean?'

'Well, if you're going to be the sensation of the arts world, you've got two mysteries to solve, not just one.'

Jessica felt her face redden again. Why did that have to keep happening? And was Noah making fun of her?

He grinned. 'I spoke to Malcolm Gladstone on the phone earlier and he told me all about the assignment he sent you on. I've known Malcolm for many years, and it seems to me the old fool is growing more and more out of touch with every day that passes. You should just — '

'Noah! Noah!' Professor Bianchi

bustled up to Jessica and Noah, looking flustered and out of breath.

'Alessandro, are you all right?' Noah said, placing his glass down and gripping the professor's arm.

'There's been a break-in at the university,' the professor gasped. 'Your office has been ransacked. It's a terrible mess.'

'What?'

'But that's not the worst of it,' Professor Bianchi said. 'Please, you have to come with me, the police are wanting to talk with you.'

Jessica watched as Noah and Professor Bianchi hurried away without a backward glance at her. Her head was a whirl of thoughts. What had happened in Noah's office that was worse than the break-in? And who would do such a thing? And why?

But above all these thoughts was Noah's last remark to her. It sounded like he had been making fun of her again, teasing her about her assignment and basically suggesting that she was out of her depth here. And what had he been about to say before he was interrupted?

You should just —

You should just what?

Leave?

Give up and go home?

Was that what he had been about to say?

Jessica decided she had had enough of the private viewing of Gagliardi's work. Putting her glass down, she glanced across the room and caught Cora looking at her, unembarrassed at being caught looking. Flustered, Jessica was the first to turn away, and she hurried out of the gallery.

There was something about that woman that unnerved her deeply.

4

Jessica hurried through the fortress, not looking properly where she was going. At the last moment she saw, on the periphery of her vision, a person in front of her, and pulled up short in surprise.

'Oh, my dear!' said the tall old man standing only inches from her.

Jessica gasped. 'I'm sorry! Are you all right?'

He put a hand to his chest. 'Well, you gave me quite a start.' He smiled. 'But yes, I'm fine, thank you.'

Jessica took a small step back and looked at him. He was wearing a charcoal-grey suit and tie and holding a walking stick. This, coupled with his shock of white hair, made him look very distinguished. He was obviously old, but he stood straight and firm, and the walking stick seemed more for decoration than as an aid to walking.

'And how about you, my dear?' he said, still smiling. 'Are you all right?'

Jessica couldn't take her eyes off him. There was something about him that fascinated her.

'I know what you're thinking,' he said, and leaned in a little closer as though about to impart some confidential piece of information. 'You're thinking to yourself, how old is this man before me? Surely he shouldn't be able to stand on his own?'

'No, no,' Jessica said, shaking her head but smiling also. 'Of course not.'

'Let me tell you,' he said, and lowered his voice a little, his eyes crinkling with amusement. 'I'm ninety-five years old.'

'Wow, that's amazing. You look fantastic.'

The old man bowed slightly. 'Why, thank you.'

She wasn't just being polite; the old man really did look wonderfully fit and healthy.

'Now, having almost just knocked me over, you really must introduce yourself,' he said with a smile.

'My name's Jessica. And how about you?'

He extended his hand. 'William. And I'm very pleased to meet you.'

Jessica took his hand and shook it. 'Are you here for the exhibition?' she asked.

'I am indeed.' William's eyes crinkled into a smile. 'I've long been a fan of Lorenzo's work, and I count my blessings that I have lived long enough to see the day when his lost portraits were discovered once more.'

'Lost portraits?' Jessica said. 'Did you know about them before they were found?'

William smiled again and held out a hand. 'Please, my dear, could you give an old man a helping hand up these steps? I could navigate them on my own, but I would feel so much better about it on the arm of a pretty young lady such as yourself.'

Well, you might be almost a hundred years old, but you're still a charmer, Jessica thought. She held out her hand, and William gripped it whilst they walked up the few steps through the doorway. In his other hand he held his walking stick. Although he tapped it against the floor as they walked, it seemed to Jessica he didn't really need it for balance or support.

'I wouldn't say that I knew about them,' he replied. 'But I was aware of the rumour that Lorenzo had painted the portraits in his declining years. And it doesn't surprise me; his passion for painting ran deep. He couldn't have resisted the call to paint again once he was released from his prison.'

'It's funny, but the way you talk about him, it's as though you actually knew him. As though you were friends,' Jessica said.

William chuckled. 'That's what happens when you devote your life to the study of someone. I have examined his work and his life so closely and for so long that, yes, I do feel as though we were friends.'

'Here we are,' Jessica said as they stepped through into the gallery space.

William stopped and gazed around the room at the paintings. 'Oh my,' he whispered. 'Lorenzo, Lorenzo.' He let go of Jessica's hand and walked over to the first painting. He gazed up at the mysterious woman, fist clenched by her side, rendered in thickly layered oils of burnt umber and strokes of white.

Jessica caught Cora looking at them. A tingle of unease ran down her back. 'William, I have to go,' she said.

'Forgive me,' he said. 'You must think I am very rude.'

'Not at all. Will you be all right here on your own?'

'Yes, yes,' William said. 'I'm meeting my great-grandson here. You go.'

And with that, he turned back to examining the painting, and seemingly forgot all about Jessica.

★ ★ ★

Jessica decided to head back to the university and find Noah. Professor Bianchi had said his office had been ransacked, but also that something even worse had happened. Jessica was worried but also intrigued. What on earth could he have meant?

As she hurried through the city centre, she suddenly found herself caught up in a crowd watching a small group of protesters march down the middle of the road, waving placards and generally blocking traffic. In their black clothing and close-cropped hair, the protesters reminded Jessica of Cora. So much so she half-expected to see her amongst the group.

Jessica tried reading a few of the signs, but they looked like they were written in German. Whatever they said, though, it looked ugly. The protesters were chanting and punching their fists in the air in some kind of salute. Many of the crowd watching them were shouting back in Italian.

Jessica turned away and pushed

through the crowd, thankful that the protest was relatively small and that there was a police presence to keep order. When she arrived at the university, she was surprised to see that everything looked normal. She had expected the grounds to be filled with policemen, tape cordoning off certain areas and hushed groups of students standing around staring wide-eyed at the unfolding drama.

But no, everything looked absolutely normal. Students wandered to and fro, clutching books to their chests, satchels hung over shoulders. Small groups of young men and women were taking advantage of the sunshine and sitting on the grass, chatting or reading.

Jessica sighed. How lovely it would be to study in this beautiful place. She missed her days at college, studying fine art. Learning about the history of art, painting, drawing, and generally mixing with others who were equally passionate about these subjects.

She entered the university building.

The restaurant was on her left, the old abbey beyond it. She paused, trying to remember which way she needed to go to find Noah's office. The university was large and sprawling, with a rabbit warren of corridors. Every time she had been here so far, she had had to ask for directions, but this time she was determined to find her way around without resorting to seeking help. Besides, it was difficult asking someone for help when they spoke a different language.

Jessica headed firmly off down the corridor she remembered walking along with Professor Bianchi yesterday and then took a left. Yes, this was the right way, she was sure of it. She stopped at a junction of corridors and examined the sign. Signs were helpful, but not so much when they were in Italian. There, that one — 'Dipartimento Artistico'. That had to be the art department, surely?

Jessica hurried down the corridor, passing classrooms and lecture halls.

None of this looked familiar, but perhaps she was simply taking an alternative route. Students passed her, carrying armfuls of books and satchels on their backs. Some had large flat black portfolio cases they carried at their sides. They were definitely art students.

Jessica turned a corner and stopped. According to the sign, she was definitely in the art department, but none of it looked familiar at all. Where had she gone wrong?

Before she could consider this question further, a door opened and a middle-aged lady hurried out. Her clothes were baggy and splattered with paint. Her face lit up when she saw Jessica. '*Ah, eccoti finalmente! Dove sei stato?*' she said, throwing her hands in the air.

'Oh, I'm sorry,' Jessica replied. 'I don't speak Italian.'

'*Tu sei Inglese? Non importa, dobbiamo affrettarci, siete in ritardo,*' the lady said, placing a hand on Jessica's back and hustling her through the doorway.

They entered a large studio. The opposite wall held a huge mirror, taller and wider than any Jessica had seen before. The rest of the studio walls were covered with drawings and paintings.

A sea of student faces greeted Jessica's entrance. A mixture of young men and women, they were all sitting on stools in front of easels, grouped in a loose circle facing an arrangement of boxes draped in cloth. Sitting on top of the draped boxes was a rather sad-looking bowl of fruit.

Jessica recognised the setup immediately from her time at college. This was a life-drawing class. All that was missing was the life model sitting in the middle, on the stack of boxes. Life models posed for up to an hour in one position, and could be clothed, but were usually nude.

'*Rapidamente ora, in fretta, è possibile ottenere cambiato qui,*' the lady said, bustling Jessica towards another door in the corner of the studio. The lady, obviously the art tutor, opened the door.

Jessica looked inside and her heart sank. This was a changing room. Which meant she was the life model!

'Oh no, I'm sorry but I'm not the model!' Jessica said quickly. 'I'm lost, that's all. This is a mistake!'

The art tutor looked at Jessica quizzically and with a slight expression of exasperation. Behind her, the students also looked at Jessica, waiting expectantly.

She should just leave. Walk out without another word. It would be terribly rude, but there was no point in trying to explain the mistake, as Jessica spoke no Italian and this lady obviously spoke no English.

But then Harrison popped into her mind, and she realised she was thinking exactly what he would have been thinking in this situation. Boring, dull Harrison. Wasn't it exactly that kind of life she was escaping from? A life without enjoyment of new experiences, without risk? This class's life model had obviously failed to turn up. That was why the students were sitting there drawing a boring old bowl of fruit. And now Jessica had a chance to be their life model. Wasn't this what she had come to Italy for? New experiences?

'All right, I'll do it,' she said, her heart performing a little stutter of excitement at the thought.

Jessica had drawn plenty of nude life models before, but she had never been one. Well, now was her chance. She closed the door. There was a gown hanging from a hook on the wall, and a little bench to sit on.

Jessica sat down and removed her shoes. She paused.

What am I doing? she thought. *Am I really going to take off all my clothes and pose in front of a group of strangers while they draw me?* She was tempted to slip her shoes back on and run from the changing room.

But this wasn't the first time she had

considered doing this. Back in her university days, she had often wondered what it would be like to be the model rather than the artist. And one or two of the other students had posed occasionally. Why couldn't she do it, too?

Come on, get a grip girl. This will be fun!

Jessica pulled off her jeans and then, without thinking about it, slipped her shirt off over her head. Sitting in the changing room in nothing but her underwear, she was suddenly struck with doubts again. *Can I really do this?* She unclipped her bra. *Of course you can!* Quickly removing the rest of her underwear before she had any more second thoughts, she then slipped on the dressing gown and opened the changing-room door. The students all turned to look at her.

The bowl of fruit had gone. The art tutor gestured her towards the stack of boxes draped with the cloth. Heart thumping with nerves, Jessica approached the centre of the room, where she was surrounded by the art students and their easels.

The art tutor held out a hand. She had obviously decided there was no point trying to talk to Jessica and was making herself understood through silent gestures instead. And this one was obvious. *Take off the dressing gown and give it to me.*

Without thinking, her body acting on autopilot, Jessica slipped off the dressing gown and handed it to the tutor. She sat down on the boxes and arranged herself into what she hoped was a suitably interesting pose.

The art tutor smiled and nodded. The students started drawing.

Jessica concentrated on slowing her breathing and emptying her mind of all thoughts about what she was doing. She was facing the mirror and could see the entire studio from her position. All of the students were focused on their work, scribbling rapidly with charcoal on large sheets of paper. And Jessica realised that although they were looking at her, studying her even, they weren't judging her or looking at her in a sexual way. She was an object to be drawn, the curves and contours of her body, the light and shade, a challenge for them. Life, to be captured on a sheet of paper. And Jessica remembered this was how she had felt in life-drawing class. It seemed she had forgotten a lot during the years she had been married to Harrison. And not just about art, but about the business of living.

Jessica settled comfortably into her pose. After a while, she knew that the pose would start to become uncomfortable as her body began crying out to move, to shift position. And then the aches and pains would start, and she would have to call on her reserves of willpower to stay still. Jessica knew this from conversations she'd had with some of the life models she had drawn in the past.

But for now she was happy. Her mind was almost in a state of meditation. Once the session was finished, she was looking forward to seeing the students' work, seeing herself captured in charcoal.

The minutes flew by, and indeed her muscles did start to ache, and Jessica became aware of a growing need to move and stretch. She resisted it, concentrating on looking at the door to the life studio she could see behind her in the mirror.

The door opened. Jessica took a sharp intake of breath. Noah stepped into the life-drawing room and walked over to the art tutor. He began talking in rapid Italian with her.

Jessica's face began heating up with embarrassment. Noah hadn't seen her yet, but if he even so much as glanced in her direction . . .

She struggled to keep still. Every nerve in her body screamed at her to jump off the boxes and run back into the changing room before he saw her. But she couldn't let the students down. They hadn't long been working on their drawings, and Jessica knew how frustrating it was if a model moved, let alone left the room!

Sitting facing the mirror, she couldn't take her eyes off Noah. He was still deep in conversation with the art tutor, and Jessica was impressed by his fluent Italian. He started to turn away as they finished their conversation, and Jessica braced herself for when he saw her. But then he stopped turning as he obviously thought of something else he needed to say.

Jessica could take it no longer. The embarrassment and suspense were excruciating. But she still couldn't jump up and run. Not only because that would be failing the students, who were still scribbling furiously away with their charcoal sticks and pencils, but also because Noah would notice the movement and see her straight away. If she stayed rock-still, she might get away with not being noticed at all. So instead of running, she screwed her eyes shut. Like a child who believes she is invisible if she closes her eyes, Jessica hid inside herself.

She could hear him talking still with the art tutor. A pause in the conversation. What sounded like the door opening, and then Noah's voice coming from that direction. He was leaving! He had to be!

She was safe. If Noah had seen her, Jessica was sure he would have had something to say. Something smart and sarcastic, probably. He wouldn't be able to resist it.

Unable to take the suspense anymore, she snapped her eyes open.

Noah was staring right at her!

They locked eyes for a moment, Jessica's face heating up even more and the warmth spreading down her neck and upper chest. She was surprised she wasn't on fire by now, she was so hot.

Noah held her gaze in the mirror for a moment and then left the studio without a word, closing the door behind him. Jessica breathed again.

As the minutes crawled by and her aches and pains grew from sitting still for so long, she began to forget about her embarrassing experience. Staying fixed in the same position began to take up all her willpower and concentration. With no clock visible in the room, Jessica had absolutely no idea how long she had been posing for the students. Surely it would be time to take a break soon? How much longer could she sit here as the aches and pains in her muscles grew in intensity?

Finally, as she was on the verge of admitting defeat, the art tutor clapped her hands and spoke rapidly in Italian. The students put down their pencils and charcoal and began chattering with each other. The art tutor approached Jessica with a smile, holding out the gown for her. Gratefully Jessica moved her stiff limbs and slipped it on.

'Thank you,' she said.

'*Ma no, grazie. Hai fatto molto bene . . . per la prima volta*,' the tutor said.

Jessica couldn't be sure, but from the look on the Italian lady's face, that twinkle in her eye, had she realised that

Jessica was not the life model after all? That this was the first time she had ever posed nude in front of a class?

And then she noticed the other woman standing at the back of the studio. And her face flushed with embarrassment again as she realised this was the model, arrived at last. The woman walked over to Jessica, smiling.

'Hello,' she said, her English heavily accented. 'Did you enjoy being the model today?'

'Oh, I'm sorry,' Jessica replied. 'I didn't mean to take your job.'

'Nonsense,' the model said. 'You did very well. You should take it up as a profession.'

Despite her embarrassment, Jessica grinned. 'Maybe I will,' she said.

★   ★   ★

After getting changed and taking a quick look at the drawings, Jessica hurried off, but not before promising to return and discuss the possibility of working with the art class again. She would have liked to have stayed longer, taken her time looking at herself depicted on paper in the eyes of the students, but Noah was on her mind.

Jessica felt strongly that she needed to find him and explain what had happened. Find out exactly how much he had seen when he noticed her sitting in the middle of the studio without a stitch of clothing on!

This time she quickly got her bearings and found Noah's office. The door was closed.

Jessica knocked.

'Go away!' Noah shouted in a gruff voice.

Oh no, Jessica thought. *He sounds like he is in a foul mood. Now what should I do?*

Before she could make a decision, the door was suddenly flung open and Noah appeared in the doorway, a look of fury on his face. When he saw Jessica, the anger disappeared and his features softened.

'I'm sorry,' he said. 'I didn't realise it was you.'

'Would you like me to leave?' Jessica said.

'No, no, come on in,' he replied. 'Although the place isn't looking its best today, as you will see.' He stood back and let Jessica into his office.

She gasped in horror at the sight that met her.

5

They went to the university café and Noah bought two coffees. Jessica didn't think she had ever drunk as much coffee as she was doing in Italy. When Noah sat down and handed Jessica her drink, his face broke out into a grin. It was as though he had been trying to hide his smile but could do so no longer, and it was very disconcerting after the look of fury she had seen on his face only minutes before.

'What?' Jessica said. 'Why are you smiling?'

'I must say you have a very lovely back,' Noah said, grinning even more.

Jessica's cheeks flushed with embarrassment. If only she could stop doing that! 'And what about the rest of me?' she said, rather primly.

'Oh don't worry, your back was all I saw,' he replied. 'The beacon of light shining from your face obscured every-thing else, pretty much like now.'

Jessica looked down at her coffee, wishing the floor would open up and swallow her whole. 'Really?' she said. 'That was all you saw?'

Noah placed a finger under her chin and gently lifted her face up again so he could make eye contact.

'Yes, really. I'm a grown man and an artist. I don't generally go around ogling the models like a hormonal teenager. As soon as I realised it was you posing, I got out of there. I wouldn't have entered the studio at all if I had known you were in there in the first place.'

Jessica held eye contact with him, trying to work out if he was telling the truth or not. Suddenly she decided he was, and he wasn't his usual jokey self now; that he was serious about this. And something shifted deep inside of her as she looked at Noah, and she wondered if he felt the same way.

Noah dropped his hand and looked

away for a second; almost as though he, too, was a little embarrassed.

'Thank you,' Jessica said.

Noah looked back at her, his eyes clear and bright. 'Have you done much modelling before today?'

'Um, no, today was my first time.'

She explained what had happened, and Noah threw back his head and laughed loudly enough that other customers in the café turned their heads and looked in his direction. 'Seriously?' he said when he had regained his composure. 'You got lost, found a life-drawing class without a model and just decided on the spur of the moment to step in?'

'Well, yes, I suppose,' Jessica said. 'I bet you think that's highly ridiculous and immature of me, don't you?'

'Oh no, just the opposite,' Noah replied, smiling. 'I think it's great!'

'Really?'

'Yes, really. Isn't that what life is all about, finding new experiences and jumping straight in there without a moment's hesitation?'

Just the opposite of Harrison, Jessica thought.

Noah suddenly grew serious, the smile fading. 'That's what I used to be like, a few years ago. Before . . . ' He fell silent.

Jessica wondered if she should say anything, tell him that she knew about his fiancée, that Professor Bianchi had told her everything. She could see now that his sometimes gruff exterior was a mask for the pain he still felt. And maybe the loneliness too. After all, devoting yourself to a life devoid of significant human relationships had to be difficult, even if it was what you wanted.

Or what you thought you wanted.

Noah was looking away again, across the crowded café. Only moments before he had been laughing, and Jessica had been amazed at how the laughter had transformed his face. Beneath that beard, Noah Glassman was a handsome-looking man; but when he smiled and laughed, something beyond even simple good looks happened to his features.

And yet, he was a troubled man. That much was obvious.

Noah's hands were resting on the table, his fingers twisting around each other. Jessica was sure he wasn't even aware he was doing it. More than anything else right now, she wanted to place her hands on his, soothe the tension and anguish he was feeling, and tell him everything would be all right. But something held her back.

Would he pull away, maybe even stand up and leave? Noah was such a complicated man, Jessica wasn't sure what his response might be to physical contact. Maybe if she just said something first. Tell him that Professor Bianchi had explained what had happened.

But before she could say anything, Noah had turned back to face her. 'Well, as you saw, my office is a terrible mess, isn't it?' he said.

Flustered by the sudden change of subject, Jessica paused a moment before speaking.

'Or hadn't you noticed?' Noah said. 'I mean, I know it's usually in a bit of a state anyway, although I hadn't thought I had let it run to ruin that much.'

'No, it's awful,' Jessica said.

Noah arched an eyebrow.

'Your office . . . I mean . . . now, not before. Oh, you know what I'm saying!'

Noah grinned, and Jessica was happy to see the smile return.

'I just can't believe that somebody would have done that,' she said.

It wasn't just the fact that somebody had ransacked Noah's office, although that had been bad enough. Drawers had been emptied and the contents strewn across the floor, chairs had been upturned and pictures torn from the walls and ripped apart. It was more like a revenge attack of some sort rather than a simple burglary.

But that hadn't been the worst of it. Over the walls, crudely painted in red, were Nazi insignia. The paint had dripped from the obnoxious symbols, running down the walls in long scarlet streaks, like blood. Jessica felt sick with fear and revulsion just looking at it. Who could do such a thing? And why?

'I know,' Noah said, breaking into her thoughts, almost as though he was reading them. 'It's sick, isn't it?'

'Do the police have any idea who might have done this?'

'No, and I doubt they'll put too much effort into finding out.'

'But that's not right! They have to do something!'

Noah shrugged. 'They've got more important things to worry about. As far as they're concerned, this is just a student prank, and it will probably never happen again.'

'But what about you? What do you think?'

Noah looked thoughtful. 'I know the students here. Not all of them, obviously — this is a large university with lots of different departments. But I know the feel of this place, and it doesn't sit right with me that any one of the students here would have done something like this.'

'Do you know who might have?'

Noah leaned back in his chair. 'Not a clue.'

'Or even why?'

Noah shrugged. 'Search me.'

Jessica's thoughts turned to the protest march she had seen on the way over to the university. 'I saw these people in town,' she said. 'Mostly young men, all dressed in black and marching through the city centre.'

'The Young Men's National Liberation Front,' Noah said. 'As sloganeering names go, it's not exactly catchy, is it?'

'What do they want; why are they protesting?'

Noah looked at Jessica grimly. 'As far as what they were protesting about today, that's the repatriation of northern Italy and specifically the Trentino region back into Austria. As for what they want, what they stand for, I don't know. Sometimes when I see their leader talking on the news, it seems to me they just want to turn the clock back to nineteen forty and fight World War Two again. As far as I can see, they're simply a bunch of neo-Nazis.'

'Then maybe it was them that vandalised your office.'

Noah shrugged. 'I suggested that to the police, but they're more inclined to think it was a student prank on the back of the protests today.'

'What are you going to do next?'

'About my office? Give it a tidy, put things back. Maybe I should think about redecorating too. What do you say?'

'Definitely,' Jessica said, and was suddenly struck with an idea. 'Why not today?'

'Why not what today?'

'Redecorate! I'll help you. We can go out and buy some paints now, and we could have it done by this evening.'

Noah sat up straighter. 'Are you serious?'

'Of course I'm serious.'

'Oh, I don't know . . . I've got a lot to be getting on with today.'

'Like what?'

Noah's brow creased as he thought about this — something else that Jessica found endearing about him.

'Well actually, now that you mention it, there's not a lot I can do until the office is back in order.'

'There you go then, that's settled! Let's go buy some paint right now.'

Noah laughed. 'I give in. You win!'

* * *

Noah decided that the red of the Nazi insignias would take too many coats of paint to cover over and that they should put wallpaper on the walls instead. They bought rolls of wallpaper and paste and headed back to the university to begin the job of tidying the office.

Noah looked at the destruction before them, and some of his enthusiasm seemed to drain from him. 'Are you sure you want to do this?' he said. 'I mean, just look at this mess. We could be here into the summer break sorting this lot out.'

'Well, the sooner we get started, the sooner it will be done,' Jessica said firmly.

Noah laughed. 'You don't mess about, do you?'

She elbowed him in the side. 'Not when it comes to sorting you men out. Honestly, if it was left up to you, this place would never get cleaned up. I can just see you now, carrying on with your work here as though nothing was wrong, sitting in this mess for years to come.'

'Hmm, you're probably right.'

'You know I'm right. Come on, we're wasting time.'

The first task was to tidy up. Working together, they sorted Noah's books and papers into some sort of rudimentary order and stacked them outside his office in the corridor. Then they shifted the furniture into the centre of the room. As Jessica was helping Noah push his desk away from the wall, it caught on something on the floor and refused to budge any more.

'We're going to have to lift it up a little,' Noah said.

Working together, they lifted the desk enough that they were able to shift it over the bump beneath the carpet and into the middle of the office, along with the bookcases and chairs.

Jessica looked at the small irregular protrusion showing through the old carpet. 'What's that?' she asked.

'A mysterious doorway into the nether regions of the earth,' Noah replied, comically waggling his eyebrows up and down.

'What are you talking about?' Jessica laughed.

'Look, I'll show you.' Bending down, he grabbed at a corner of the carpet and easily pulled it back.

'Do you think maybe you need a new carpet?' Jessica said.

'This old thing was here when I

moved a few years back, and it was probably here when Gagliardi was painting his mystery portraits. Look at this.'

Jessica joined him in the corner. Set into the dusty concrete floor was a large wooden trapdoor. The protrusion beneath the carpet had been the iron pull ring. 'What's down there?' Jessica said, looking at Noah wide-eyed.

Noah shrugged. 'Nobody knows.'

'Seriously?'

'Look — it's locked.' He bent down and tugged at the iron ring. The door didn't shift at all.

'And nobody's thought to go and find the key, or break the door open?'

Noah was squatting by the trapdoor and Jessica joined him. 'Alessandro seems to think it's an old well, last used by the abbey, but probably sealed up before they closed down.'

'But surely someone must have been curious enough to try and take a look?'

'Well, this carpet was laid down long before I came here, and nobody has mentioned taking a look. It just kind of sits there, all forgotten underneath the carpet and my desk. Every once in a while I might catch my toes on the ring, but apart from that I don't think about it, and I'm sure everybody else has forgotten all about it too.'

Jessica shook her head. 'I'd love to know what's under there. Can't we get it open?'

'Maybe,' Noah said, smiling. 'But not today. We've got a lot left to do yet.'

Jessica turned and looked at the rest of the furniture waiting to be shifted, and sighed. 'I suppose you're right.'

She soon forgot about the trapdoor in the floor as they continued with the job of sorting Noah's office into some kind of order. When they were ready to start wallpapering, she stopped work.

'Is something wrong?' Noah asked.

'Aren't we supposed to have a wallpaper-pasting table?'

'I knew we'd forgotten something.'

'I suppose we could lay the paper on the floor.'

'Or better still, we could just slap the paste straight onto the walls.'

'Will that work?'

'Let's find out, shall we?'

'You're the boss,' Jessica said.

Noah laughed. 'I don't believe that for one minute!'

They worked hard together, and the hours flew by. For Jessica, this was the first time she had been alone in the company of a single man, at least since the split with Harrison. Being with Noah felt right. It felt comfortable. And Noah didn't seem to be minding her company, either.

By the time they had finished papering all of the walls, covering up the obscene symbols daubed in red paint, the light was fading outside. Jessica wiped a forearm across her forehead. 'Wow,' she said. 'Look at that. We did it.'

'We certainly did,' Noah replied, standing back and admiring their work.

'And we didn't do too bad a job either, did we?'

'We did a great job.' Noah glanced

her way, his eyes crinkling with amusement. 'If the bottom ever drops out of the life-modelling business, you could always start up as a painter and decorator.'

Jessica laughed.

Noah held up a hand. 'Hey, high five, Miss Matthews.'

They high-fived each other, and Jessica said, 'All we have to do now is move your furniture back into place, and then the stuff from the corridor back into your office.'

'Forget that,' Noah said. 'After all that work, I'm starving. Aren't you?'

As if on cue, Jessica's stomach let out a rumble of hunger.

Noah grinned. 'Well, that answers that question. Come on — I know a place where we can grab something to eat, and it's on me. I can sort the rest of this stuff out tomorrow.'

'Okay, if you insist,' Jessica said.

'I do insist. And I'm the boss, remember?'

Jessica just smiled.

'Hey,' Jessica said as the waiter left, having taken their order. 'I've just remembered, you never told me what you were going to say.'

Noah scrunched up his forehead as he thought about this, and repeated what Jessica had just said in an exaggeratedly slow fashion. 'You never told me what you were going to say. Sorry, I don't get it.'

'Back at the Gagliardi exhibition,' Jessica said, and leaned forward. 'You told me you'd spoken to Malcolm Gladstone about my . . . ' she held up her fingers and made inverted commas with them, ' . . . project, and then you called him a doddering old fool — '

'Now hold on, I didn't call him doddering,' Noah exclaimed, holding a hand up in protest.

' — and you said that he was out of touch and that I should just . . . ' Jessica paused, waiting for Noah to speak.

'Just what?' he said finally.

She sighed with exasperation. 'Well, I don't know. You never finished your sentence. That was when you found out your office had been ransacked.'

'Oh, I remember now,' Noah said. 'I was about to say you should just ignore Malcolm and his promises that you will be the sensation of the arts world. He's such a dramatist. You need to just concentrate on your work, on investigating the mystery behind these paintings — for you, not for Malcolm and his latest sensational news story for his magazine.'

'Oh, I see,' Jessica said.

'Why, what did you think I was going to say?'

'Oh, I don't know,' she replied, hiding her embarrassment behind her drink as she remembered that she had thought Noah was telling her to just give up and go home.

'In fact, I was thinking we should work on this together,' Noah said. 'I mean, do you have any idea where to start in finding out who the mystery woman is in the paintings?'

'Are you serious?'

Noah looked hurt. 'Well, I was only trying to be helpful when I asked if you had any idea where to start. I didn't mean to say — '

'Don't be silly! I meant, are you serious about us working on this together? That would be wonderful!'

'Really?'

'Of course it would!'

A slow smile of pleasure crept across Noah's face. It wasn't his usual cocky smile; in fact, it was almost vulnerable in its tenderness.

There was a moment of silence between the two of them. Sitting in the pizza restaurant, a charming old building in the Piazza Duomo, in the flickering, warm light of a candle set on the table, Jessica realised this was a perfect setting for romance.

It seemed Noah came to the same realisation as he leaned back in his chair and glanced around the restaurant.

'Where on earth is our pizza?' he

said, picking up his glass and taking a deep swallow of his drink.

Jessica laughed. 'We've only just ordered it!'

'Have we?'

This was fascinating, seeing a side of Noah that Jessica hadn't expected to exist. Was it only yesterday they had first met, and he had been rude and insulting? Now here he was, buying her dinner and acting like a giddy teenager. Not that Jessica exactly felt mature and grown up. And romance wasn't what she had come to Italy for. Absolutely not.

'So what else do we know about Gagliardi and his mysterious portraits?' she said, changing the subject.

Noah coughed and placed his drink on the table. Coke, Jessica noticed. Was Noah off the alcohol for the moment?

'Not a whole lot, unfortunately,' he said.

'What about where they were discovered?'

'A cellar in a house on the outskirts

of the city. They'd been down there for decades, and were in pretty bad shape. The university spent a lot of money on cleaning them up and restoring them, once they realised what they had on their hands.'

Jessica already knew this, but she loved hearing Noah talk and so let him carry on.

'The house had been owned by the same family for over a hundred years, and simply passed down through the generations. It was only because the old man who died in the house was the last of his family that the place was put on the market, and when it came time to clear out all the rubbish in the cellar the paintings were found.'

'Did this family have any connection with Gagliardi?' Jessica asked.

'None that we know of,' Noah replied, thoughtfully. 'And, as far as we know, there's no one left to ask.'

'Do you know why Gagliardi was imprisoned in the fortress during the war?'

Noah shook his head. 'Nope. Another mystery to solve. And, although he only started his portraits of the young woman after his release from his prison when the war ended, and the Allies took back control of Northern Italy from the Germans, I can't imagine he met any beautiful young women during his imprisonment.'

'But this period of captivity obviously had a marked effect upon him.'

'Yes, it did, which is partly why I decided to hold the exhibition of his paintings at the Palazzo delle Albere. It just seemed right, somehow.' Noah paused, deep in thought for a moment. 'Hey, I just realised — I bet you haven't seen the room he was kept in during the war, have you?'

'No,' Jessica said. 'But I'd love to. Maybe tomorrow.'

Noah waved a hand dismissively. 'Forget about tomorrow. Why not tonight, after we've eaten?'

'But won't the fortress be closed?'

'Yep, but locked doors don't mean a

thing when you have a key,' Noah said, smiling.

'You have access to the fortress?' Jessica said, astonished.

'Of course I do. I'm the exhibition curator. I need access at all times of day and night.'

They were interrupted as the waiter returned with their pizzas. Jessica couldn't believe how large they were, served on black pieces of slate and sizzling hot. Jessica had ordered a capricciosa topped with mozzarella, tomato, mushrooms, artichokes, cooked ham, and olives. It looked delicious, and she remembered how hungry she was.

'Let's eat up,' Noah said. 'And then we can go exploring the Palazzo delle Albere. What do you think?'

'I think that sounds like a perfect plan,' Jessica replied, and dived into her pizza.

6

The sight of the fortress sent an involuntary shiver through Jessica. It looked ominous and forbidding in the darkness of the evening. The sky was clear, full of stars shining bright against the purple of the night. In the distance, the snow-capped peaks of the mountain tops were still just visible. It was enough to spark romantic notions in the most hardened of cynics. But the Palazzo delle Albere was a monstrous shadow looming over them as they drew closer to it.

'Are you sure this is a good idea?' Jessica whispered.

'Why are you whispering?' Noah whispered back.

'I don't know. Why are *you* whispering?'

'You started it.'

Jessica sighed. This was getting

nowhere. 'I don't know, it just doesn't seem right to talk too loudly.'

'You're acting as though we're criminals.'

'Maybe that's because I feel like one,' Jessica hissed. 'Are you sure you have permission to do this?'

Noah chuckled. 'Stop worrying. We're fine.'

They walked up the wide gravel driveway to the entrance. On either side of them were large expanses of lawns bordered by colourful flowers. Jessica couldn't imagine this was how the fortress had looked when it was originally built as a defence for the region. Nor would it have looked like this when Gagliardi was imprisoned in its walls during the Second World War. But now it was a museum, and it depended on its continued upkeep and existence as a historic attraction.

Noah had already had to unlock a door in the large iron gates to let them into the grounds, and then they had crossed a moat. Now, as they approached the fortress itself, Jessica was struck by another thought.

'Won't there be an alarm system? We might set it off!'

Noah stopped walking and slapped the palm of his hand against his forehead. 'Oh my goodness! I hadn't thought of that! What are we going to do?'

Jessica looked back at the entrance to the fortress grounds. 'Maybe we already set one off when we came through the gate! The police could be on their way already!' She looked back at Noah and saw him grinning. 'You're teasing me, aren't you?'

'Maybe, a little.'

'There are no alarms at the gate, are there?'

Noah shook his head, still grinning.

Jessica sighed in exasperation. Back at the restaurant, she had seen a tenderer, more thoughtful side to him. But now he was being silly again, and seemed intent on teasing her at every opportunity he got.

'You're right, there is a security system set up at the fortress,' he said, his smile softening as though he realised he was going too far. 'But I have the security code to deactivate it, so we'll be fine.'

'All right, as long as you're sure,' Jessica said.

'I promise, Scout's honour.' He held up his hand.

'I'm not sure I believe you were ever a Scout,' Jessica replied. 'And even if you were, I bet they would have kicked you out for being a disruptive influence.'

Noah put his hand against his chest. 'Ouch, I'm hurt. How could you say such a thing?'

They continued walking up the drive until they got to the fortress entrance. Noah produced a huge old-fashioned key and inserted it into the lock.

'Are you ready?' he said.

'Just get on with it,' Jessica whispered.

He unlocked the door and pushed it

open. A beeping started up, and Noah crossed the foyer to a panel set into the wall. He punched in the security code and the beeping stopped. 'There we go, all done,' he said, turning to face Jessica.

She switched on her torch and played the light across the walls and the floor. Noah switched on his torch too.

'If we're not criminals breaking into the fortress, why did you insist we bring torches with us?' she asked.

'Always with the questions!' Noah cried out in mock exasperation. 'Because I'm not sure I want to be switching all the lights on in the fortress for just the two of us. And besides, if the place is lit up like a beacon in the night, we might end up drawing tourists, and I don't want to spend my time here explaining that no, the fortress isn't open and — '

'We are breaking and entering and could they please refrain from calling the police?' Jessica said, interrupting him.

'And not having time to look at the

room where Gagliardi was imprisoned, was what I was going to say,' Noah finished.

'Let's do it quickly then. This place is giving me the creeps.'

Noah led the way through the fortress. Jessica expected him to take her straight to where Gagliardi had been imprisoned during the war, but instead he led her to the exhibition. She didn't ask why. It just seemed right somehow.

They walked up and down the vast hall, studying each of the portraits in the light of their torches. Gagliardi's young subject looked even more mysterious now. Sometimes she seemed almost to disappear into the frenzied layers of chiaroscuro laid on thick, whilst in others she was a bright, shining centrepiece to the painting. But in all of them her fierce determination was plain to see, and that right hand curled up tight into a fist by her side.

What did it mean? With no other frames of reference in the paintings, it was impossible to tell what her expression and posture meant. Jessica had the feeling they would never find out who the mysterious young woman was.

'Let's take a look downstairs, shall we?' Noah said, startling Jessica a little. She had become so lost in the painting that she had almost forgotten where she was and who she was with.

'Downstairs?' she whispered. 'I thought we would be going upstairs into one of the towers.'

'Nope, Gagliardi was kept in the dungeon,' Noah said, and that grin appeared again. 'You're not scared of going there, are you?'

'Of course not.'

She followed him out of the exhibition hall and down a wide set of stone steps. At the bottom they turned back on themselves and into a narrow, low corridor.

More like a tunnel, Jessica thought. She could feel the damp in the air emanating off the stone walls. They were obviously underground now.

'Here we are,' Noah said, his voice sounding strange in the enclosed space. He pushed a door open and they stepped inside.

The dungeon where Gagliardi had been imprisoned was a little larger than Jessica had expected, but not much. The floor was just grit and dirt, the stone walls dark with damp. Above them, the arched stone ceiling seemed to weigh heavily down upon them. Noah had room to stand upright in the middle, where the ceiling was at its highest, but if he moved to either side he had to duck.

'How long was Gagliardi kept prisoner here?' Jessica asked

'Just over two years.'

'Wait, are those chains set into the wall?' She shone her torch at the stone wall with the iron rings protruding from it and a short length of chain hanging from the rings.

'Yes, Gagliardi was kept chained down here; at least that's how his rescuers found him,' Noah said sombrely. 'It's possible that he was tortured, too.'

Jessica turned away from the iron rings. 'That's horrible!' she exclaimed. 'Who would do such a thing, and why? He was an artist, not a . . . a spy!' She thought about this for a moment. 'Was he?'

'Not that we know of, no,' Noah replied. 'And I think it's highly unlikely. After all, how many monk-turned-artists do you know of who became spies? By all accounts, Gagliardi was the mild-mannered, reclusive, gentle type. Hardly material for World War Two spying, wouldn't you agree?'

'So why did they torture him?'

'Again, we don't know. The fortress was occupied by the Germans as their central headquarters in Trentino, not as a prison camp. The only clue we have is that Legend Niedermeyer allegedly visited the fortress regularly during the latter part of the war.'

'Legend Niedermeyer?' Jessica said.

'Who on earth was he?'

'A rather vicious Nazi official who never quite achieved the notoriety he should have, even though he was never caught and nobody knows what happened to him. Ironic really, considering the fact that he named himself Legend because he believed that was what he was, a legend in his own time.'

'But I didn't know any of this.'

'Hardly anybody does. It was only after the discovery of Gagliardi's late-period work, and when I decided to curate the exhibition, that I started digging around for a little more information on him. Because Gagliardi had never been an artist of note before, nobody had bothered to look into his life.'

Jessica shivered. 'I think I'd like to leave.'

'I don't blame you. I think I feel the same way,' Noah said.

Seemingly without thinking about it, he took her by the hand to lead her out of the dungeon. His grip was firm but gentle, and she didn't resist. They walked up the set of wide stone steps together, their torches lighting their way.

At the top of the stairs, Noah let go of her hand. A pang of disappointment spiked Jessica in her chest. Despite his sometimes infuriating manner, there was also a tender, caring side to him. And Jessica couldn't help but wonder if she was starting to fall for him, despite her promise to herself that she had come to Italy to reground herself in her life, not for romance.

But Noah was such a mystery to her. Had he held her hand just now because he was starting to feel the same way, or just because he could tell she was unsettled and disturbed? He was looking away from her, towards the open doorway leading into the exhibition hall, and she was able to examine him without him realising. Yes, definitely handsome, and much younger than he first appeared underneath that beard. She wondered if he had always had a beard, or if it had grown after his fiancée's death, when he had let himself go.

Jessica so wanted to tell him that she knew his secret; that Professor Bianchi had told her all about his loss. She wanted to hold him in her arms and comfort him. Maybe now would be a good time. They had spent the day and the evening together, and she felt that a bond had started to grow between them. Maybe now was the perfect time to reach out and connect with him.

Screwing up her courage, she said, 'Noah — '

'Shh!' he hissed. 'There's somebody in the exhibition hall!'

This time it was Jessica who took hold of Noah's hand; grabbed it, really. He didn't push her away or let go, just continued staring at the open doorway.

'Switch off your torch,' he whispered.

They both killed the light from their torches and were immediately swamped in darkness. After a few moments, when her eyes had become more used to the dark, Jessica realised she could see the grey illumination of the open doorway into the exhibition hall. She stood completely still, holding onto Noah's hand.

Was there really somebody in the hall? she hadn't seen or heard anything yet. Noah could have imagined whatever it was that made him think there was somebody out there. These ancient buildings had to be full of creaks and groans as they settled from the day's heat into the evening's coolness.

Just as she reached the point where she was about to ask Noah if he was sure he had heard an intruder in the hall, Jessica saw a bright beam of torchlight cut across the open doorway. Her heart started beating fast and hard, and then she heard a whisper and saw a second beam of light. There were two of them! Noah's grip tightened on her hand.

She saw two shadowed figures come into view through the doorway. They were both at the opposite end of the hall, their torches playing over the paintings on the walls. But, Jessica realised, if they turned and shone their torches through the doorway, they would see Noah and Jessica right away.

As if reading her mind, Noah beckoned to her to follow him. Still holding on to her hand he led her to one side of the doorway, out of sight of the intruders. Safely pressed up against the wall and hidden from view, Noah bent down and put his lips to Jessica's ear.

'Stay here,' he whispered. 'I'm going to try and get a better look; see what they're up to.'

Jessica shook her head and opened her mouth to implore him not to, but he put his fingers over her lips and silenced her.

'Don't worry, I'll be careful,' he said.

Even in the tension of the moment, Jessica felt a thrill at the sensation of his warm breath on her ear, and the touch of his fingers on her lips. What a ridiculous time to be feeling such things!

Noah eased himself around her and towards the doorway. She watched him as he edged up closer and peered around the door frame. He stayed that way for a long moment and then pulled back. Jessica was suddenly overcome with a powerful urge to take a look for herself.

'What are they doing?' she asked, her voice little more than a breath.

'They're looking at the paintings, one by one,' Noah replied; and although she could hardly see him in the gloom, she could tell by the tone of his voice that he was puzzled. She heard noises from the gallery, sounds of things being moved around and low murmurings of conversation.

Noah eased himself back into a position where he could see what was going on. After a few long moments he turned back to Jessica. 'They're taking the paintings off the walls,' he whispered. 'I'm going to call the police.'

Jessica let out a quiet sigh of relief. This was what they should have done immediately.

Noah pulled his mobile from a pocket and activated it, shielding the glow of the screen with his other hand. Just as he was about to tap in the number for the emergency services, they heard a ripping sound from the exhibition space.

'Oh no!' Noah shouted. 'They're destroying Gagliardi's paintings!' Shoving the mobile into Jessica's hands, he said, 'Call the police, now!'

Jessica almost dropped the phone as she watched Noah dash through the doorway and disappear from sight. She followed him.

The first thing he did was find the light switches. The gallery was suddenly flooded with light, and Jessica threw up her hands to shield her eyes from the dazzling glare. She was blinded, but she was sure the two intruders were too, and that that had been Noah's plan. But, dazzled as he had to be, Noah was running, dashing through the hall to save his beloved paintings.

Squinting at the phone, her eyesight only just starting to return to normal, Jessica heard a crash and a cry. She looked up and saw Noah falling to the floor, holding his left thigh. Had he been shot? Were the intruders armed with guns?

And the number for the emergency services! Noah hadn't told her. What was it?

Climbing to his feet, Noah set off at a run again, although he was limping now. Jessica's vision had cleared enough that she could see the two intruders had escaped. Noah ran through the doorway at the opposite end of the hall, leaving her all alone with Lorenzo Gagliardi's paintings.

She looked at the phone again, feeling helpless. Because she hadn't used it for a few seconds, it had gone to sleep. She reactivated it and the password screen appeared.

Oh no, she thought. *Now I can't*

even get access to his phone to try and find the emergency number to call for the police!

Then she saw the word 'Emergency' in tiny lettering in the bottom left-hand side of the screen. She tapped it, and the mobile automatically took her to the telephone screen, and the word 'Calling' appeared. Relief flooded her system. Now all she had to hope for was that the operator spoke English.

'*Carabinieri, Pronto Intervento,*' a voice spoke on the mobile.

'*Non parlo Italiano, parli Inglese?*' Jessica said, dragging out the only Italian she knew and hoping for the best.

Suddenly Noah appeared by her side and took the phone from her. He spoke in rapid Italian with the operator for a while and then disconnected the call. 'The police are on their way,' he said grimly.

'Are you all right?' Jessica asked anxiously. 'Did you ask for an ambulance, too?'

'An ambulance?'

'They shot you in the leg! I heard it. I saw you falling down holding your leg.'

Noah chuckled. 'No, no. I ran smack into a table, caught my thigh on the edge of it and gave myself a dead leg.'

'So they didn't have a gun?'

'Not as far as I'm aware, no. But they did have a knife. Look.'

He led Jessica over to the stack of paintings that had been taken off the wall. One of them lay on the floor, the canvas roughly slashed diagonally in half. Noah squatted by the painting but didn't touch it. Jessica knelt down beside him.

'Why would anybody do such a thing?' Jessica said.

Noah shook his head. 'I don't know. And I wonder . . . '

Jessica looked at him. 'What?'

He turned to face her, his features set in a grim expression. 'Are the two vandals who did this the same ones who ransacked my office?'

Jessica turned cold at the suggestion. What on earth was going on?

7

The *polizia* kept them for some time at the fortress, and Noah had to explain several times what he and Jessica had been doing there before they were satisfied. It was late by the time they were finished, and Noah took Jessica straight back to her lodgings. She was surprised to see lights still on in the house and wondered if Stefania was sitting up, worried about where she had got to.

Noah walked her up the drive to the front door. Stefania's house was big and modern and set amongst beautifully tended gardens on the outskirts of Trento city centre. They were higher than the city, and the glow of the old buildings down below looked charming and wonderful.

'Well, what a day this has been,' Noah said.

'Quite,' Jessica replied. 'First your office was broken into and turned upside down, and then the fortress!'

Noah suddenly looked a little embarrassed. 'Well, that wasn't quite what I was thinking of.'

'You weren't?'

'No.'

Jessica waited for him to say something more, to explain what he meant. But he just stood there, looking at her.

'So what were you thinking of?' she asked, eventually.

'Well, um, the first thing I wanted to say was, well, to apologise for how rude I was to you yesterday.'

'That's all right; you already did that.'

'Well, yes, I suppose I did. But it was under duress, if I'm honest.'

'What do you mean, under duress?'

Noah looked even more embarrassed now. He coughed and looked away for a moment. 'Well, Alessandro basically threatened me with the sack unless, as he said, I rejoined the human race and started acting like a decent person again.'

'Really? He said that?'

'Yes.'

'And that's the only reason you apologised to me, because you didn't want to lose your job?'

'Um, well, um, yes.'

Jessica thought about this for a moment. She'd already known this to a certain extent, although she hadn't realised Professor Bianchi had threatened Noah with the loss of his position at the university. So why did she suddenly feel so very disappointed?

'But that's why I wanted to apologise again!' Noah said hurriedly. 'My first apology didn't mean much, if I'm honest. But this one, this one does.' He took hold of both her hands. 'Jessica, I'm so sorry.'

She looked up into his eyes. Unlike the fortress, which had been so dark and gloomy, here the night sky was clear and blazing with stars, which gave the darkness a certain special luminosity. Jessica felt she could almost see as well as during the day. Noah's eyes glistened in the night light, and she could tell that this time he was being sincere. But what did that mean? Could it be that he was starting to feel the same way she did?

'So why the change of heart?' she asked him softly.

'Like I said, it's been quite a day,' he replied. 'And mainly due to the amount of time we've spent together. I feel I've got to know you a little better today, Jessica.'

He leaned in closer, and Jessica remembered how his breath felt as it had caressed her ear, and the touch of his fingers, and she wondered what his lips would feel like on hers. She arched her head back a little as he drew closer.

'It's strange, but I never thought I would fee — '

The door opened.

'Well, there you are at last! I thought you were never coming back!'

Jessica turned, her whole body reeling with shock. 'Mum!' she exclaimed. 'What are you doing here?'

'I thought I'd surprise you with a visit,' Jessica's mother said. 'That wasn't exactly the welcome I'd been expecting though, I must say.'

She looked at Noah as though just noticing him for the first time. Jessica saw her expression soften as she took in his slightly roguish appearance, and the closeness with which he was standing to Jessica.

'Oh, hello,' she said, a coy smile creeping across her face, as she held out her hand. 'I'm Angela, Jessica's mother.'

'I'm very pleased to meet you,' Noah said, shaking her hand.

Stefania appeared behind Jessica's mother. 'Are you all right?' she asked. 'We were getting worried about you.'

'Yes, we're fine,' Jessica said.

Before she could explain about the night's events, a small shape bolted outside and a familiar voice shouted, 'Hey you! You wanna fight?'

Noah burst out laughing. Tomasso stood in his Spiderman pyjamas with his fists clenched, staring up at Jessica. She knelt down and put up her fists too.

'Hey you! You wanna fight?' she repeated.

Tomasso grinned and turned and fled back inside as his mother shouted after him, 'Tomasso, you should be in bed!'

'What did I just see?' Noah said, still laughing.

'It's the only English he knows,' Stefania explained. 'He learnt it off some TV show he loves to watch.'

'Well, I'm not sure how useful that will be in daily life, but it sure entertained me,' Noah said, chuckling.

'Come inside, all of you. Have you heard there's been a break-in at the fortress?' Stefania said.

'We know all about the break-in,' Jessica said. 'We were there.'

They went inside, and Stefania's husband, Fabrizio, introduced himself to Noah, almost seeming to size him up as to whether or not he was a suitable candidate for Jessica, as the two men shook hands. Jessica noticed that her mother could not stop looking at Noah, that coy little smile flitting occasionally across her face. Jessica cringed inwardly. It seemed everyone was jumping to the conclusion that Noah and she were a romantic couple.

Stefania made drinks whilst Jessica and Noah told them all about the night's events. Jessica's mother kept interrupting, asking questions and throwing in comments. *Here we go,* thought Jessica. *How am I ever going to spend any time alone with Noah now that my mother's here?*

'But who would do such a senseless act of vandalism?' Stefania said when Jessica and Noah had finished telling their story.

Noah took a sip of his coffee and ran a hand through his tousled hair. 'Beats me. The whole thing makes no sense at all.'

'What an adventure!' Angela said, clapping her hands together. 'And how romantic, the two of you fighting off those terrible criminals together!'

Jessica shot her mother a look, one that she hoped communicated the message that she wanted her to shut up. 'But why are you here?' she said, in an attempt to change the subject.

Jessica's mother huffed. 'I thought you would have been pleased to see me.'

'Of course I'm pleased to see you. It was just such a shock to find you here. Why didn't you tell me you were coming out?'

'Because I knew you would do your best to try and persuade me not to,' Angela said. 'But I also knew if you were out here on your own, you'd do nothing but work, writing up that silly essay for that magazine.'

'Mum!' Jessica groaned, and mentally kicked herself. Why did she always turn into a sulky teenager in front of her mother?

'Well you would, and don't tell me otherwise. It's about time you had some fun in your life again, now that you've got rid of that awful cheat, Harrison.'

Noah arched an eyebrow. 'And Harrison is . . . ?'

'Jessica's husband,' Angela said, a look of distaste crossing her face, as though she had just stepped in something smelly.

Noah's eyebrow shot even further skyward. 'Husband?'

'Ex-husband,' Jessica said firmly.

'And a close relation to the lizard species if you ask me,' Angela said. 'Not at all like you, Noah.'

Noah smiled. 'That's very kind.' Jessica wasn't sure if he was joking.

Angela leaned forward in her seat. 'Now do tell me, Noah — are you married?'

Jessica cringed again. Why did she have to do this? And what would Noah say? Would he mention his fiancée and the accident?

'Oh no, most definitely single. That's me, a confirmed bachelor,' Noah replied.

Jessica couldn't help but glance

sharply in Noah's direction. A confirmed bachelor? What did he mean by that? What about the moment they'd had outside on the doorstep? Oh, if only her mother hadn't interrupted!

'Now I find that hard to believe,' Angela was saying. 'A handsome young man like you, single?'

Noah shifted slightly in his chair and ran a hand through his hair again.

'I'll bet you have to fight the women off with a stick, don't you?'

'Mother!' Jessica hissed.

'Oh no, not really,' Noah replied, shifting in his seat again. 'I'm much too devoted to my art to have time for any . . . um . . . romance.'

'Nonsense!' Angela said. 'There's always time for a little romance. Life's simply too short. Why, I remember when Jessica used to — '

'Mother!' Jessica snapped. 'Will you please stop? I'm not twelve years old still, you know.'

Angela tutted and said, 'That might be true, but you certainly act like a twelve-year-old sometimes.'

Biting down on a cutting reply, Jessica looked away for a moment. They were in danger of having a proper argument if they carried on like this. Jessica loved her mother dearly, but sometimes she could be so very infuriating.

'Anyway, you're so much nicer than Jessica's last husband,' Angela was saying. 'Oh, he was so boring. Not like you, I'm sure, Noah.'

Noah shifted in his seat again and coughed. 'Oh, I don't know. I'm pretty boring myself, to be honest.'

'I don't think you're quite telling me the truth there, are you?' Angela said, wagging a finger at him. 'Why, I know what you men are like. I remember when Angela brought home her first boyfriend and he — '

Unable to take the tension she was feeling anymore, Jessica stood up and said, 'It's late, and I'm tired. I think I'm going to go to bed.'

'That's a good idea,' Noah said, also

standing up. 'I think I'll join you.'

Stefania giggled, and Noah flushed, suddenly realising what he had said. 'I mean at home, in my own bed,' he stammered. 'Alone, obviously.'

Jessica had never wished more that the floor would open up and swallow her whole.

Everyone stood up then, and good-byes were said, and Noah left without a backward glance at Jessica. As she stood in the doorway and watched him walk down the road towards his car, Jessica wondered if she would even see him again.

Because she had the feeling there was a distinct possibility that Noah Glass-man might lock himself in his office and not emerge until Jessica and her mother had left Italy for good.

★   ★   ★

'That sounds so exciting!' Caterina exclaimed, and turned to her mother. '*Perché non mi hai svegliato? Ho perso tutte le emozioni!'*

Sunshine streamed through the large windows. Jessica smiled as she ate her breakfast. Poor Caterina had slept all through the excitement last night.

'English, please, while we have our visitor,' Stefania said. 'And the reason I did not wake you is because you need your sleep, and I didn't want to worry you with stories of break-ins.'

Tomasso grinned, as he had been awake and out of bed.

Hmm, Jessica thought. *You obviously understand more than you can say.*

Caterina turned on her brother. 'Why are you so happy? It's not fair that you were up and I wasn't!'

Tomasso, still grinning, raised his fists and said, 'Hey you! You wanna — '

'Tomasso!' Stefania said sharply. 'Eat your breakfast, please, or you'll be late for your piano lesson.'

Tomasso did as his mother said, but he was still grinning.

'What are you doing today, Caterina?' Jessica asked. It was a Saturday and there was no school.

Caterina rolled her eyes. 'I have homework to do.'

'History?'

'No, English. I have to describe something in English, something unusual with detail, like scenery or the plot of a movie. It's boring.'

Jessica thought for a moment. 'What about a painting?'

Caterina looked at her. 'Maybe. But what sort of painting?'

'How about a portrait of a mysterious woman, painted by Lorenzo Gagliardi?' Jessica looked at Stefania. 'If it's all right with you, I could take Caterina into town to the exhibition. Perhaps she can help me solve the mystery of who the mysterious young woman is in Gagliardi's paintings.'

'*Oh, per favore mamma! Posso per favore?*' Caterina blurted out, her eyes wide and pleading.

Stefania laughed. 'English, Caterina, English. And yes you can, as long as that is all right with Jessica.'

'Of course it is,' Jessica said, smiling. She looked back at Caterina. 'We'll have fun, right?'

'Right!' Caterina said, and gave her a thumbs-up.

And it will be fun, Jessica thought. *It'll do me good, too. Maybe take my mind off Noah for a while.*

Initially, Jessica had thought about going back to the university and helping Noah move his furniture back into his office. But after last night's embarrassing encounter with her mother, and her blatant attempts at matchmaking, Jessica had decided Noah would much prefer to be on his own this morning. She didn't want to crowd him.

Besides which, she still wasn't entirely sure how he felt about her. Last night, after their exciting encounter with the intruders in the fortress and then their closeness under the stars in the night sky, it had been easy to think that her romantic feelings were being reciprocated. But now, in the bright morning light, the whole thing seemed ridiculous.

Jessica still felt the same way about Noah. In fact, she could hardly stop thinking about him.

But did he feel the same way about her? Or had she been imagining the whole thing?

* * *

Noah spent the morning shifting the furniture and his books back into his office. He had hoped to see Jessica this morning, but it seemed obvious to him now that she wasn't going to turn up anytime soon. Which was a shame, as he was growing very fond of her.

Noah hadn't expected to feel this way about a woman again after he lost Sarah. It had been years since her accident, but he still felt the pain of her absence every day. Maybe if he had got on with his life after a shorter period of mourning, he might not feel this way now. But no, he had chosen to withdraw into himself, to separate himself from society. Of course he lived and worked in a busy city, and he lectured in front of students. But all of that was superficial.

He could act out the performance of his life as the visiting lecturer in art every single day with ease. He'd had enough practice over the years. It was only when he was on his own that he could let the mask drop, and be who he really was.

The other day, meeting Jessica for the first time, had been unfortunate. The mask had slipped in front of her, and he had been rude and unpleasant.

Noah sat down at his desk, and the chair creaked, threatening to send him flying. Why did he even keep the old thing?

But he knew the answer to that. Because Sarah had bought it for him. Originally it had been for their home, a luxuriant piece of office furniture for his workspace in their house. But then she had died, and now he took it everywhere with him, even paying to have it shipped over to Italy when he got the position at the University of Trento. The only problem was, it was falling apart. What would he do when it finally broke beyond repair? It was his last link to Sarah.

Noah propped his elbows on his desk and put his face in his hands. Perhaps it was best if he didn't see Jessica again. He wasn't ready for romance.

He never would be.

8

The gap on the wall, where the painting had been that was sliced open with a knife, was painfully obvious to Jessica. The thought of being here last night with those two intruders in the fortress sent a shiver through her.

A lot of people stopped to gaze at the blank space as though it was a work of art itself. The city had been abuzz with news of last night's break-in, and now it seemed that the Gagliardi exhibition was more popular than ever. Although Jessica hated the thought that someone could so callously wreak damage on a work of art, it looked like the notoriety might give Gagliardi some much-needed exposure.

'She's beautiful,' Caterina said, staring up at one of the paintings. 'But she looks . . . '

Jessica waited for Caterina to find the

words she was searching for.

' . . . I don't know,' she finally said, sounding disappointed that she couldn't express herself properly.

'I know what you mean,' Jessica said. 'There's something about her, isn't there? Something not quite right.' Maybe it was the way in which Gagliardi had painted his mysterious subject. Or that she looked so fierce and determined, almost angry.

'She looks as though she is about to have a fight with someone,' Caterina said. 'Or maybe she is in a battle.'

Something about what Caterina said rang a tiny bell in the back of Jessica's mind. She tried chasing that thought down, but it disappeared like a wisp of smoke before she could catch it.

Caterina sat down cross-legged on the floor and started sketching the painting in a pad she had brought with her. She had been doing this with each of the paintings she had looked at, and Jessica had been impressed at her talent for drawing.

Jessica looked at the painting again whilst Caterina drew. The young girl was right — there was definitely something off about the painting; about all of the paintings. Something to do with the woman, the object of Lorenzo Gagliardi's gaze. But try as she might, Jessica could not pin down what it was.

She realised that Caterina had stood up again and was talking to her. 'And the paint is so thick,' she was saying.

'That's a painting technique known as *impasto*,' Jessica said.

'In paste?'

Jessica laughed. 'Yes. It's a technique where the artist lays the paint on in thick daubs so that it stands out in ridges. Can you see how those ridges of paint add highlights and shadows to the painting, creating an illusion of depth?'

'Oh yes!' Caterina said, and moved closer to the painting. 'I want to touch the painting, feel the bumps.'

'I know what you mean,' Jessica said. 'But we're not allowed. The natural oils in our skin would start to destroy the paint if enough people ran their fingers over the paintings.'

Caterina turned away from the Gagliardi portrait to say something else, but her eyes were drawn over Jessica's shoulder to the room behind.

'Who's that?' she said.

Jessica turned and looked.

Cora. Again, the sight of that woman unsettled Jessica. She was once more wearing all black, in stark contrast to her white skin. The severe cut of her hair emphasised her sharp cheekbones and tight mouth. She was talking to a man, and he looked so similar to Cora that Jessica suspected they were brother and sister. He wore a black shirt open at the collar, and black trousers, but it was impossible to tell the colour of his hair as his head was shaved bald. Jessica could see a tattoo creeping out from under his shirt and onto the lower half of his neck. And his appearance was just as unsettling for Jessica as Cora's.

'I don't know,' Jessica said in answer to Caterina's question. 'But let's not stare, shall we?'

They moved along, pausing to study each of Gagliardi's portraits.

'But each one is so different!' Caterina exclaimed.

The painting they were currently examining had a much softer appearance than the previous thickly layered portrait.

'This technique is known as *sfumato*,' Jessica said, 'meaning, to evaporate like smoke.'

Caterina laughed. 'Now you are translating Italian to English for me!'

'Do you see how the contrast between light and shade is softened by a misty, smoky appearance? This was a technique invented by Leonardo da Vinci, and he used it most famously in his portrait of the Mona Lisa.'

'But why did Gagliardi use so many different styles to paint this same woman over and over again?' Caterina asked.

Jessica smiled. 'We don't know. And that's part of the mystery.'

'Look at them, Willem — how jolly exciting for them,' a voice spoke behind Jessica.

She whirled around on the spot to find Cora and her companion standing right behind them. So close that they must have heard everything that was said.

Caterina stepped back and bumped into the painting. Her eyes were wide with apprehension.

'Do you think they are art detectives?' Willem said. 'On the trail of a shocking mystery?'

His accent was strong, but Jessica couldn't work out what it was. 'Excuse me,' she said, concentrating on keeping her voice firm before the direct and confrontational stares of Cora and Willem. 'You interrupted a private conversation. Can I help you in any way?'

Cora only smiled. Up close, Jessica could see that she wearing a thin line of black lipstick. Was there no other colour she liked apart from black?

Cora reached out and took Caterina's sketchbook from her. She leafed casually through the pages, quickly looking at each drawing in turn. 'So, have you found out yet?' she said, ignoring Jessica's question. 'Do you know who the woman in the painting is, and why Lorenzo spent his final years obsessively painting her over and over again?'

Cora and her brother, if that was who he was, pressed in closer. Jessica had to step back, uncomfortable in their presence, and she also bumped into the painting.

'Careful,' Willem said. 'You don't want to damage the precious work of art.'

And he smiled too, if you could call the thin line of teeth appearing in his face a smile. It could just as easily have been a snarl. A sudden tension gripped Jessica's insides, tightening her stomach.

It was you two! she thought. *You were the ones in the gallery last night! You were the ones who sliced the painting apart! But why?*

'Don't worry about me,' Jessica said. 'I'm not likely to damage the painting, as I haven't got a knife on me.'

What had she said that for? If they really were the intruders who vandalised the Gagliardi portrait, the last thing she should be doing was antagonising them.

'Are you making an accusation?' Cora said, arching a perfectly shaped black eyebrow. 'You won't find what you're looking for.' She moved even closer to Jessica, until they were almost touching. 'Cleverer people than you have been looking for decades, and they still haven't found it.'

What was she talking about? Who were these people she was referring to, and what was it they had been looking for?

Jessica turned her face away. She couldn't bear to be so close to this woman. Caterina looked like she was about to cry.

The poor girl, Jessica thought. *This wasn't what she had expected to happen going out with me this morning.*

Jessica didn't know what to do or say next. She wasn't even sure what Cora and Willem wanted, or why they were acting in this threatening way. Had Jessica done something to offend them?

'You should leave now.'

Noah! Relief flooded through Jessica's body as she heard his voice.

Cora and Willem drew back. Noah stepped into Jessica's view and used his presence to herd them further away.

'Oh, Noah,' Cora said, her voice smooth and yet still full of menace. 'Since when did you start keeping the company of children?'

'What do you want, Cora?' Noah said, ignoring her question. 'Why are you here?'

'For the same reason everybody else is, it seems,' Cora replied. 'To discover the identity of Lorenzo Gagliardi's mysterious subject.'

'Well I suggest you go about your business and stop threatening people, especially young girls, or I might have to call the police.'

'Come, Cora, let's leave,' Willem said, smiling that humourless cold smile of his.

Noah looked at him. 'And who's this clown? Your taste in boyfriends is getting poorer and poorer.'

Cora threw back her head and laughed. 'Noah, this is my brother! You remember Willem, don't you?'

The colour drained from Noah's face. 'Leave now,' he hissed, 'before I most definitely call the *carabinieri*.'

'Yes, Willem, let's go, shall we?' Cora said, turning to her brother. 'Noah is so boring these days, keeping the company of children.' She cast a contemptuous glance at Jessica as she said this, and tossed Caterina's sketchbook to the floor.

The two of them turned and walked

away. As they left, Cora glanced back, pouting her lips and blowing a kiss to Noah. He turned his back on them.

'Are you both all right?' he said.

Jessica started trembling as the tension left her body. She concentrated on pulling herself together for Caterina's sake. 'Yes, I'm all right,' she replied, putting an arm around Caterina's shoulders. 'How about you?'

'Those two are weird,' the young girl replied. She bent down and picked up her sketchbook.

'Weird and more than a little frightening,' Jessica said.

Caterina looked up at her. 'I'm okay. I felt safe when your boyfriend arrived.'

Jessica glanced at Noah and blushed. 'Oh, he's not my — '

'We're just good friends,' Noah interrupted.

'I think I should get Caterina home,' Jessica said.

'Oh no, can't I look at some more of the paintings?' Caterina exclaimed. 'I haven't seen them all!'

'No, we should get back. I'm worried that those two will return and threaten us again, and your mum needs to know what happened.'

'But Noah could stay with us and protect us!'

Noah shifted his weight from one foot to the other. 'I, erm, I've got a lot to get on with if I'm — '

'Oh please!' Caterina cried. 'If I see more of the paintings, I might be able to work out who the mysterious woman is.'

Despite still feeling a little shaken at the encounter with Cora and her brother, Jessica couldn't help but smile.

'Well, it would be nice for Caterina to see the rest of Lorenzo's paintings, and if you're not too busy . . . '

Noah sighed, but he was smiling too. 'All right, I will escort you two young ladies around the exhibition; and then we should take you back home, Caterina. Deal?'

'Deal!' Caterina said, grinning.

* ★ ★

As it turned out, Noah not only escorted them around the exhibition, but also took Jessica and Caterina to a nearby pizzeria for lunch. He hadn't meant to; he had pretty much decided that he was going to keep out of Jessica's way as much as possible for the rest of her stay. It had seemed to him that he was foolish to be having these feelings towards her, and not just because he didn't think he was ready for romance again.

When he looked at her and saw how beautiful and alive she was, how she lit up any room she was in, he couldn't believe that she would have any feelings at all towards him. It was true — he had let himself go in the years since he lost Sarah. In fact, if she could see him now, she would be shocked at the change in his appearance.

Noah had only come to the Gagliardi exhibition this morning because, as its curator, he had to. He had hoped to not encounter Jessica; had planned on keeping out of her way if she was there. But then he had seen Cora and that thuggish brother of hers intimidating Jessica and Caterina, and he'd had to step in straight away. And now here he was, despite having promised himself to keep out of her way, taking Jessica out for lunch!

Jessica said something, breaking into his thoughts.

'I'm sorry?' Noah said.

She laughed. 'You were a million miles away, weren't you? I said, how do you even know that woman?'

'Who, Cora?' He sighed. 'We had a brief relationship, many years ago.'

Jessica had been about to eat a slice of pizza, but now she had to put it down as she stared at him in surprise. 'Seriously? You and her?'

Noah nodded. 'We were students, and it only lasted a few weeks. She wasn't so strange back then, although she was still different. And she had all these bizarre ideas about the universe and the powers within it, and how the human race should be aligning itself to the spiritual centres of the elephants who carry the universe on their backs through time and space.'

'That's just silly!' Caterina said, her mouth full of pizza.

Noah grinned. 'Okay, I made up the bit about the elephants, but she did have some fairly way-out ideas.'

'So what did she believe?' Jessica asked.

Noah shrugged. 'I'm not sure. It was all mumbo jumbo to me. But at the end of the day, it all had something to do with the improvement of the human race, and not in a good way. The more she explained her philosophy to me, the more uncomfortable I became. I mean, we weren't talking racial purity or anything like that, but it was drawing close. And she was starting to mix with some people who had more extreme views than she did. So I ended it.'

'And you knew her brother too?' Jessica said.

'I wouldn't say I knew him, exactly, but I met him a couple of times.' Noah shook his head slowly. 'He's younger than Cora, and he was a vicious thug, in and out of jail all the time. He's lost a lot of weight — probably drugs I should think — and I hardly recognised him.'

Noah took a bite of his pizza. Talking about Cora, about the past, had brought back the feelings of loss he had for Sarah. Also, he couldn't help but wonder what Jessica thought of him now that she knew he and Cora had once been a couple. Although Noah would hardly describe their time together as romantic. It had been one of the most awkward relationships of his life, which was partly why he had cut it off so quickly.

His mood was starting to drop, and he knew he needed to change the subject before he was overcome with sadness.

But it was Jessica who took him by surprise and pulled him back to the present when she said, 'Cora and Willem were the ones who broke into the fortress last night.'

Noah almost dropped his slice of pizza. 'What? What on earth makes you think that?'

'They told me,' Jessica said, and then paused. 'Well, they as good as told me. Willem told me to be careful of the paintings, and that I didn't want to damage them.'

'That's hardly — '

'It was them,' Jessica said, her voice firm. 'I know it was.'

Noah took a bite of his pizza and chewed thoughtfully. 'Maybe it was,' he said. 'But why?'

* * *

Jessica couldn't stop thinking about Noah and Cora, as Noah drove her and Caterina back to Stefania's house. How could he have even thought about going out with her? She had to keep reminding herself it was a long time ago, and that the relationship had only lasted a few weeks.

But even so, her head was spinning with thoughts. Was this relationship with Cora after the death of his fiancée, or before? And why was Cora here now? Was it just because of the Gagliardi exhibition, or did she intend to try and reignite her relationship with Noah again?

At least Jessica was sure about one thing. From the way he had talked about Cora, Noah had no intention of letting that happen.

There was another demonstration going on in the city centre today, this one by the Anti-Young People's National Liberation Front. The sight of all the people out, with their placards and chanting their slogans, saddened Jessica. Trento was such a beautiful, peaceful city at all other times. Why did there have to be such hatred in the world?

When they arrived back at Stefania's home, Caterina jumped out of the car.

'Thank you for the lift!' she said, smiling. 'And for protecting me from that awful woman.' She ran up the drive to the front door.

'Well, the encounter with Cora and Willem doesn't seem to have had a lasting effect upon her,' Noah said.

'I hope not,' Jessica replied. 'I still find it hard to believe that you and that woman were a couple once.'

Noah sighed. 'I wish I'd never told you.'

'Really? But why?'

Noah shifted in his seat. 'Oh, I don't know. Just seeing her now, knowing what she's like, what she's turned into, makes me wonder what I was thinking of at the time.'

Jessica's thoughts turned once more to the tragedy in Noah's life. He still didn't know that Professor Bianchi had told her about his fiancée. And she had the distinct feeling that Noah never talked about it; that he had kept his feelings of loss under wraps for all these years.

Maybe now was the moment to bring it up. Perhaps, after what they had been through together in the last couple of days, Noah would feel able to open up to her.

'Jessica! Jessica!'

She groaned. *Once again, mother, your timing is impeccable*, she thought.

Angela bustled up to the car. Jessica lowered the window. It occurred to her that she should have been getting out; that Noah had been dropping her off, not picking her up. But somehow it didn't feel right to get out of the car just yet. There was unfinished business between the two of them.

'Why didn't you tell me you were going into Trento?' Angela said, looking accusingly at Jessica through the open car window.

'You were sleeping!' Jessica replied. 'I didn't want to disturb you.'

'Well, I'm up and dressed now, as you can see,' Angela said, and smiled sweetly at Noah. 'Good morning, Noah. You don't mind giving an old lady and her daughter a lift, do you?'

'Of course not,' he replied.

'But we've only just got back!' Jessica said.

'Well you shouldn't have been so impatient to go into town in the first place.' Angela opened the car door. 'Now come on, jump out and get in the back. You know how I get car sick if I sit in the back seat.'

Jessica groaned. Noah had his head turned away, looking out of the driver's-side window. Jessica had the distinct feeling he was hiding his amusement, which infuriated her even more.

'What's wrong with you?' Angela said. 'You're acting like a silly teenager!'

That's because you're making me feel like one, Jessica thought as she climbed out of the car.

9

Noah drove back into Trento and parked at the university. Jessica's mother had talked at top speed all the way, whilst Jessica sat silently in the back. There was no point trying to say anything. Once her mother got talking, nothing and no one could interrupt her. It wasn't even as if she actually had anything to say, either. That woman could talk non-stop about absolutely nothing for hours on end.

By the time they parked, Jessica's anger at her mother's interruption into not just her day, but her entire trip to Italy, had bubbled and boiled so much inside of her that she felt like a pressure cooker about ready to explode.

'What's wrong with you, Jessica?' her mother said as she climbed out of the car. 'You've been very quiet in the back.'

Jessica swallowed the sarcastic reply that had risen automatically to her lips. *You were so busy talking, you never left enough space for anyone else to get a word in!* 'I'm just tired, that's all,' she said.

'Well, I'm not surprised, gallivanting until all hours of the night and then up again with the larks this morning. You're meant to be on holiday, having a rest.'

Noah's mobile blared into life and he pulled it from his pocket. 'It's Alessandro,' he said, and turned away from them as he answered the call.

'I thought perhaps the two of you could show me around the city,' Angela said. 'It just looks so pretty, and you both make such a lovely couple.'

'Mother!' Jessica hissed. 'We aren't a couple!'

'Well you should be. He's such a lovely man.' Angela paused a moment. 'He could do with shaving that beard off, though, and a haircut too.'

Jessica couldn't help but roll her eyes,

even though she'd had exactly the same thoughts.

'Now don't you roll your eyes at me like that young woman,' Angela said. 'Honestly, I don't know what's come over you this morning.'

You have, that's what, Jessica thought.

Noah finished his call and turned back to face them. 'Seems I'm a wanted man,' he said. 'Alessandro has asked if I could pop into the university to talk to a visitor about Lorenzo Gagliardi. They're waiting for me now.'

'Ooh, how exciting! Do you think it's the police?' Angela said.

He smiled. 'Nothing so dramatic, I'm afraid. Just an appreciator of Gagliardi's work who wants to talk about these late-period paintings of his.'

Jessica wanted to say something to Noah, but she was stuck for the right words. It looked like they were about to go their separate ways, and she didn't know when she was going to see him again. If only her mother wasn't here!

But then Noah saved the day. 'Why

don't you take your mum and show her around the university while I meet this visitor, and then when I'm finished I'll come and find you and we can head into the city centre together?'

'That would be lovely,' Angela said before Jessica had even had the chance to open her mouth.

Noah smiled — and did Jessica catch a hint of laughter in his eyes as he looked at her?

They headed into the university building, where they were met by Professor Bianchi and his visitor. Jessica recognised him immediately.

'How lovely to meet you again,' William said, extending his hand and shaking hers in greeting.

'You two know each other?' Noah asked.

'We met at the gallery yesterday,' Jessica replied, smiling.

'And it seems our shared appreciation of Lorenzo Gagliardi has brought us together once more,' William said.

Jessica noticed he was holding his

walking stick, but again he didn't seem to need it for support, but more as a decoration. A fashion statement almost, in a curious sort of way.

Introductions were made all round, and Angela looked as though she was in seventh heaven as William took her hand and bowed slightly. He was very English and very dashing, Jessica noticed. Almost a man out of his time.

'William has come to ask about the period of Gagliardi's life spent here, at the abbey,' Alessandro said.

'And also consult the foremost expert on Lorenzo Gagliardi,' William said, looking at Noah.

A small crowd of students bustled past them, laughing and talking.

'Why don't we go to my office, where it's quieter?' Noah said. He turned to Jessica. 'I'll come and find you when I'm done.'

Jessica's stomach did a tiny back flip at those words, and she smiled.

* * *

'It's obvious the two of you are completely infatuated with each other,' Angela said as they walked to the abbey.

'Mum, I've only just met him!' Jessica protested.

'There you go — my point exactly,' her mother said, as though that settled an argument.

Jessica looked at her, mystified. 'What do you mean?'

'You and Harrison were friends for the longest time before you became a couple, and then you were engaged for even longer. I always had my suspicions he wasn't right for you, and I think you felt the same way too.'

Jessica stopped walking. For once it seemed her mother had said something that mattered. Jessica and Harrison *had* spent a long time delaying their marriage. There had always seemed to be a practical problem to overcome before they could tie the knot.

And what an apt saying that was, too. Now that she thought about it, hadn't marriage to Harrison seemed like being tied to him? Was her mother right? Had Jessica always secretly doubted her love for that man? Had she always suspected that it would not work out?

'I'm sorry if I'm dragging up all the hurt and the messiness again,' Angela said. 'And I know you think I'm an old busybody who should keep her nose in her own business.'

Jessica opened her mouth to protest, but her mother stopped her.

'Now don't go trying to say otherwise, because it's true. But I'm only saying these things because I don't want you to make the same mistakes again. Anyone can see that you and Noah are completely besotted with each other. Now, I don't know what's wrong with him that he can't seem to make the first move, so that means it's up to you.'

'Mother,' Jessica said weakly.

Angela held up her hands. 'I know, it's not the sort of thing you want to talk about with me, but I had to say something. Now, why don't you show me this abbey, and then I'll potter into town and leave you and Noah alone for the rest of the day.'

★   ★   ★

Jessica walked down the stone steps into the crypt, followed by her mother. Angela had to take the steps slowly and carefully. The red and blue spotlights illuminating the stone walls gave the vaulted crypt a beautiful and eerie atmosphere.

At the opposite end to the steps, in their archway, stood the twin statuettes of Julian the Hospitaller. Jessica had been telling her mother about the legend and its connection with Gagliardi as they wandered around the abbey ruin. Now that Jessica was looking at the two identical statuettes once more, there was something about them that bothered her. Something she couldn't quite put her finger on.

Jessica held out her hand towards the

statuettes. 'Mum, meet Julian the Hospitaller.'

Angela shuffled closer to inspect the ceramic figures. 'Which one is Julian?' she asked.

'Both of them.'

'Oh. I thought maybe they were — '

'Twins, I know. I thought the same.'

'What a creepy little place this is,' Angela said, looking around. 'And I don't really understand your interest in it. I mean, I thought you came to Italy to look at those paintings, not explore church crypts.'

'Before he was an artist, Lorenzo Gagliardi was a monk, here at this abbey,' Jessica explained.

'And then he was captured by the Germans in the war, and after that he took up painting?'

'No, not quite,' Jessica said. 'For many years Lorenzo was a monk here, until he lost his faith. It may well have been the struggle in himself between his faith and his artistic calling that led him to renounce his life here. Once he left the abbey, he devoted himself to his art, and it was about another decade before the start of the war, and then the occupation of Italy by the Germans, and Lorenzo's capture.'

'Oh, I see,' Angela said, turning back to the statuettes and leaning down to inspect them. 'And this is meant to be him, is it?'

Jessica sighed inwardly. She could tell her mother had no idea how fascinating this all was to her.

'Well, I'm still not sure I see why you're so interested in this little man and his silly story,' Angela muttered. She straightened up and began turning around again. As she turned, the edge of her handbag, hanging from her shoulder, almost brushed one of the statuettes.

'Careful!' Jessica exclaimed. 'You almost knocked it over!'

'Oh, don't be silly,' Angela replied. 'I was nowhere near it.'

'I just want you to be careful, that's all.'

'Of course I'm being careful,' Angela snapped. 'Anyway, I'd quite like to go back upstairs. I'm finding it quite creepy down here, especially with those horrible statues watching me all the time.'

'Hello down there!' Noah shouted from the top of the steps.

Angela jumped and let out a tiny little yelp of surprise. Her handbag knocked one of the statuettes and it toppled from its place. It hit the floor and shattered with a sharp crack.

Jessica covered her face with her hands. 'Oh no!'

Noah ran down the steps, head bowed under the low stone ceiling. 'Is everyone all right?' he said.

'We're both fine,' Jessica said from behind her hands, 'but I'm afraid Julian isn't.'

Noah squatted down by the fragments of pottery that had once been Julian the Hospitaller. 'Oh dear,' he said.

'I'm so sorry, but you startled me,

shouting down into the crypt like that,' Angela said.

Noah picked up Julian's head, the only part of the ceramic statuette that hadn't shattered. 'We've still got this, at least.'

'And you've still got the other one,' Angela said slightly indignantly.

'I can't believe it,' Jessica moaned from behind her hands. 'Was it very old? Was it worth very much?'

'I've no idea,' Noah replied. 'It's been here a long time, I know that much. Hey, what's this?'

Jessica finally took her hands away from her face and saw Noah sifting through the shattered pieces with his finger. He picked something up and lifted it before his face.

'It's a key!' Jessica said.

Noah held it higher so they could all inspect it. The mortice key was large and ornate, the handle decorated in curlicues and scrolls.

'Where did that come from?' Angela asked.

'It must have been inside the statuette,' Noah replied. 'I wonder how long that's been there.'

'Wouldn't someone have heard it rattling around inside?' Jessica said.

'No, this thing was solid clay.' Noah continued to gaze at the key. 'I wonder which door this fits.'

Jessica snapped her fingers. 'The trapdoor in your office! It has to be!'

Noah looked up at her, a slow smile creeping across his face. 'How do you fancy trying this key in the lock then?'

She grinned. 'You just try and stop me.'

* * *

The three of them crowded into Noah's office. The first thing they had to do was move the desk again. Once more, as Noah and Jessica dragged it across the floor, it caught on the iron ring beneath the carpet, and they had to lift the desk slightly to get it over.

'Why is your desk heavier today?'

grunted Jessica. 'Has it been overindulging since we last shifted it?'

Noah laughed. 'No, it had been emptied when those two burglars ransacked it. It's full of my stuff now.'

Jessica let go of the desk and stood up straight. 'Wait a minute! Do you think Cora and Willem broke into your office?'

Noah stood up straight too whilst he thought about this. 'Hmm, I don't know. I'm still not entirely convinced they were the ones who broke into the fortress and vandalised that painting. For all her faults, Cora is an art lover. It's not in her nature to go around mindlessly slicing open canvases.'

'Will you two stop talking and get on with opening this trapdoor?' Angela said. 'I want to see what's down there!'

'We'd best do what your mother says,' Noah said, giving Angela a cheeky smile. 'I reckon she'll cut up rough if we don't listen to her.'

'I certainly will! Now come on, get this carpet up.'

Noah pulled back the carpet, revealing the heavy wooden trapdoor set into the concrete floor.

'What I don't understand is, if this thing is so old, how come it's set in concrete?' Jessica asked.

'Don't forget, the university is built on the abbey grounds,' Noah explained. 'It wasn't just the ruins of the main abbey building that had to be protected, but other parts of the site too. When they built over this part of the university, the contractors probably just set the concrete around the trapdoor.'

'I still can't believe no one has bothered to take a look down there,' Jessica said.

'Well I can,' Angela snorted. 'The way you two are standing around gassing, we won't get to take a look down there ourselves unless you get a move on.'

Noah grinned. 'Mrs Matthews, would you do me the honour of unlocking the trapdoor?'

Angela had been holding the key like

a sacred talisman the entire time Jessica and Noah had been uncovering the trapdoor. She had hardly taken her eyes off it, as though it might come to life and bite her.

'Really? You want me to . . . ?'

Noah swept his outstretched arm towards the trapdoor in a grand gesture.

'Go on, Mum,' Jessica said, her voice hardly louder than a whisper.

All of a sudden the room seemed to have gone very quiet. It was as though the rest of the university didn't exist anymore; that there was just this office, and the three of them in it. And the solid wooden trapdoor in the floor.

Should we be the ones to open this? Jessica thought. *Perhaps we should wait and tell Professor Bianchi, who can alert the proper people. Maybe we'll damage something by opening it up ourselves, something of great historical value.*

Angela was already walking closer to the trapdoor, and Jessica knew it was too late to stop now. Whatever lay beneath that wooden door was calling to them, all three of them, and she knew that none of them could wait any longer.

How long had that key been kept hidden within the statuette of Julian the Hospitaller? And why? There had to be something hidden deep underground beneath the abbey. Something of value, surely.

Angela stood by the trapdoor, the large ornate key in her hand. She bent down and pushed it into the lock. She tried twisting it clockwise, but it wouldn't budge. Next she tried twisting it counter-clockwise, but still the key wouldn't move.

'I don't think it's the right key,' she said, standing up straight. She left it protruding from the lock.

'It has to be,' Noah said, squatting down beside the trapdoor. He tried twisting the key both ways, but still it would not move.

'Careful,' Jessica said. 'We don't want

to get it jammed in there, or broken.'

Noah looked up at her. 'Maybe this isn't the key for this door, after all. Maybe there's another door somewhere in the university that we don't know about. Or maybe it's just a key, a random key put inside that statuette of Julian for a joke.'

'What kind of joke is that?' Jessica said.

'Well, we've fallen for it, haven't we?'

Jessica squatted down beside him. She pulled the key from the lock. It slid out easily enough. She gave it a quick, rough wipe on her shirt, leaving behind dark stains, and then slid the key back in the lock again.

Still the key would not budge as she tried twisting it first one way and then the other. 'I know this key is for this door, I know it is!' she exclaimed.

Noah put a hand on her shoulder. 'I know you're disappointed. I am too. But like I said, it's probably just an old well down there, and nothing more exciting.'

Jessica was hardly listening to him, her thoughts tumbling over one another so fast she couldn't keep up with them. Despite Noah's doubts, she was convinced that it was Cora and Willem who had vandalised the painting in the fortress. And she was also convinced that they were the ones who broke into Noah's office. The Nazi graffiti was probably nothing more than a smoke-screen. They had been searching for something, and Jessica was starting to wonder if this trapdoor, or at least what might be hidden beneath it, was part of what they were looking for.

'This lock looks too big for the key,' Jessica said.

'There you go, it's the wrong key,' Angela said.

Jessica inspected the ornate key carefully.

Come on, come on, you've got a secret, I know you have. Tell me what it is, show it to me. Her eyes roamed over the curlicues and intricate designs of the handle. So complex, so unique.

Almost like a . . .

Jessica looked up at her mother and Noah. 'This is the right key,' she said. Turning it around so that she was holding it by the lock end, she slowly inserted the handle into the keyhole. It was a perfect fit.

'I don't believe it,' she heard Noah whisper.

Carefully, Jessica turned the key towards the edge of the door, as though she was locking it. After all, if the key was reversed, then surely the mechanism would work in reverse too?

Her instincts were right. The tumblers fell into place with a dull clunk.

'Jessica, you're a genius!' Noah yelled.

She grinned up at him.

'Go on then, open it,' Angela said, her voice trembling with excitement.

Jessica closed her fingers around the iron ring, gripping it firmly. 'Here goes,' she said, and pulled.

10

Jessica and Noah squatted either side of the square hole in the floor, peering down into the darkness. Just beneath the square lip of the trapdoor opening, the shaft widened out, becoming a circular stone wall dropping into the gloom.

'Looks like Alessandro was right after all,' Noah said. 'It was a well.'

'Looks that way, doesn't it?' Jessica said, trying to keep the note of disappointment out of her voice.

'If only we had a torch.'

Angela rustled around in her handbag. 'You could use the one on my iPhone.'

'Mum!' Jessica said, looking up at her mother. 'Since when did you get yourself an iPhone?'

'I might be old, but that doesn't mean I have to stay stuck in the past,'

Angela said primly. 'I'll have you know we even have a colour TV in our house, and one of those new-fangled washing machines.'

'Sorry,' Jessica said, smiling, and taking the phone from her mother's outstretched hand. She switched on the torch function and held it out over the hole. The light, strong as it was, barely penetrated the darkness. Jessica stretched further into the hole.

'Be careful,' Noah said.

'Yes, don't drop my phone,' Angela said.

'I was thinking more of you,' Noah said to Jessica. 'I don't want *you* dropping down there. We don't know how deep it is.'

Jessica lay down on her front, only her head and one arm over the square hole in the floor. She lowered the phone into the stone shaft as far as she could. The torch function illuminated the sides of the circular shaft, but couldn't reveal how far the drop extended.

Jessica pushed her hair off her face

and wiped at her eyes. She was getting hot and sweaty with all the exertion and the excitement. As she was about to straighten up again, she noticed some gaps in the stonework, picked out by the bright light of the mobile. 'Look at these,' she said to Noah.

Shifting position on the floor, Noah looked where Jessica was indicating. The holes in the stonework were spaced regularly at alternate intervals, descending into the gloom.

'I don't know about you, but they look like hand- and footholds to me,' Noah said.

Jessica wiped sweat off her forehead with her free hand. 'Like a ladder,' she said.

'Exactly,' replied Noah.

Jessica wiped more sweat off her face. 'We could climb down there and take a look.'

'Absolutely not,' Noah said. 'Not until we get hardhats, head torches and some safety gear.'

'Killjoy.'

'It might not just be joy that ends up getting killed if you try climbing down there without being harnessed up. We have no way of knowing how deep this well is, or even if there's still water at the bottom.'

'I suppose you're right,' Jessica sighed. She rotated the mobile, trying to get a good look at other sections of the stone wall. The iPhone slipped from her hand, slick with sweat, and dropped silently down into the darkness. The smack as it hit the ground echoed up from the bottom of the well.

'Oh no!' Jessica looked at her mother, her face screwed up in anguish. 'I'm sorry!'

'Oh, Jessica,' Angela sighed. 'You always did have butter fingers.'

'Look, it's still working,' Noah said.

Everyone peered into the hole. The bottom of the shaft was faintly illuminated with the white light of the mobile's torch.

'Well, at least we know the well isn't filled with water still,' Noah said.

'Is that an opening in the side?' Jessica said. 'Looks like it might be a tunnel.'

'Could be,' Noah said.

'Oh come on!' Jessica exclaimed. 'We can't stay up here now! We should go down and take a look.'

'Absolutely not,' Noah replied firmly.

'I'll be careful, I promise,' Jessica said solemnly.

'There is no way on this earth I am letting you go down there without safety equipment,' Noah replied. 'And that's it.'

★ ★ ★

A small group of staff and students had gathered around Jessica and were watching her as she lowered herself feet first into the stone shaft. Once word had got around the university of the discovery, it seemed everyone and their mother was popping in for a look, and Noah's office was soon crowded beyond its capacity.

'I've never been this popular in my whole career,' he said ruefully.

Jessica had known she could wear Noah down and get him to agree to letting her explore the shaft. She could see it in his face, that curiosity — wondering what was down there, where it led. Once he had agreed, though, she still had to wait until they found Chad, an American student, who was also a climber and a caver. He agreed to run back to his digs and grab a harness and a helmet along with a head torch. Jessica could barely stand the wait as every passing visitor took a turn to peer over the edge of the hole in the floor and into the depths.

Professor Bianchi was like a bottle of fizzy pop as he bustled around the crowded office, he was so excited. 'I'd forgotten all about the trapdoor in your office!' he kept saying to Noah. 'How wonderful that you found the key!'

'It wasn't me, Alessandro,' Noah replied. 'You should be thanking Jessica's mother.'

'Oh, my dear!' Alessandro exclaimed, and enveloped Angela in a hug.

For the first time in Jessica's life, she saw her mother blush and stay uncharacteristically silent. Maybe it was the fact that nobody had yet explained how the key was found, and that the prized statuette of Julian the Hospitaller was now an unsolvable jigsaw puzzle, its pieces scattered across the crypt floor.

After what seemed like forever, Chad had finally returned with his safety gear. He quickly and expertly harnessed Jessica up and attached her to a safety rope which he looped around the legs of Noah's desk. 'I'll feed out the rope as you climb down,' he said. 'If you slip and fall, I'll be able to halt your drop.'

Jessica nodded, her stomach churning with excitement and anxiety.

'Are you all right to do this?' Noah said. 'I can go down there if you're not sure.'

Jessica punched him lightly on the arm. 'No way! You just want to be the first one down there, get all the glory.'

Noah laughed and held his hands up in surrender. 'All right, you win! I'm nothing but a glory-hogging thrill seeker!'

But when it came time to lower herself into the dark, Jessica almost had second thoughts. This was exciting, the adventure she had come out to Italy to have. But she hadn't quite expected to be lowering herself underground in the ruins of an ancient abbey. Who knew what she was going to find down there? She gingerly placed her feet in the gaps in the stonework, whilst holding onto the rope. Chad was strong; had the rope looped around his back and was feeding it out slowly whilst supporting her.

When Jessica had lowered herself enough that her chin was level with the floor of Noah's office, she was able to slip her hands into the gaps in the stonework. There was a ridge in each of them, which helped her grip them.

She looked up at Noah, who was gazing back down at her.

'You okay?' he said.

'Absolutely,' she replied. 'These holes in the wall, they definitely feel like foot- and handholds.'

'Just be careful.'

She nodded, gave Noah one last smile, and lowered herself into the darkness.

★　★　★

The handholds were spaced regularly enough that there were plenty of them. Jessica would have felt confident climbing down here without the safety gear, but she knew it was a sensible precaution. One slip and she could fall to the bottom and crack her head open.

She kept going down, hand by hand, foot by foot, until suddenly, almost unexpectedly, her feet were on solid ground. Letting go of the handholds, Jessica realised she was trembling, with excitement or nerves she wasn't sure. She craned her head back. The square opening above her was filled with faces peering down.

'I'm at the bottom!' she shouted.

'Are you okay?' Noah asked, his voice echoing around the stone shaft.

'I'm fine.'

'What about my phone?' her mother shouted.

Jessica bent down and picked it up from where it was lying on its front. She turned it over and wiped soft clay-like mud off the screen. Remarkably, it looked undamaged. Jessica activated it and turned off the torch function. The battery was down to fifteen percent. She slipped it into a pocket and shouted, 'It's still working!'

The ground felt soft and yielding beneath her. When Jessica moved her feet, there was a soft squishing noise, and she felt like if she stayed still for long enough she would start to slowly sink. Looking at the ground, her head torch illuminating everything she turned to, she could see she was standing in mud.

'What can you see down there?' Noah asked.

'The ground's muddy, but I can't see where the water might be coming from,' Jessica replied. 'It's almost as though the water is seeping up through the ground.'

She touched the stone walls just to make sure, but they were dry, just as she had thought. The water was definitely seeping up.

'I think you're right,' she said. 'This might have been a well once, but it dried up.'

Jessica turned around in a circle, examining the perimeter of the stone wall where it met the ground.

And there was the opening she had suspected she could see from Noah's office. She bent down and tried to get a good look inside, to see if it might lead anywhere. Although the opening looked big enough for her to fit in, it was too low for her to be able to see much without actually getting down on the ground on her hands and knees.

Oh well, she was already hot and sweaty and her clothes smudged with dirt from the climb down here. Getting mud on her hands and knees seemed the next logical step. After all, it wasn't as if she was trying to impress anyone with her glamour and style, was it?

The mud was sticky and cold to the touch, seeping between her fingers and quickly covering her knees as she peered into the opening in the wall.

Her breath caught in her chest. It wasn't just a shallow opening in the wall as she had feared.

It was a tunnel!

★   ★   ★

Noah had to stop himself from pacing up and down in his office. He had to bite back the urge to yell at everyone to get out and leave him alone. For the last few years, this place had been his sanctuary, his refuge, his hiding place.

And now look at it. There were currently more people in here right at this moment than had probably ever visited in the whole time he had been employed by the university. How had that happened? His eyes fixed on the open trapdoor. He knew perfectly well how this unlikely scenario had come about, and whose fault it was.

Jessica Matthews had been like a bomb exploding in his ordered, secluded life. She had destroyed the protective shell he had built around himself in the years since Sarah had died. And now he doubted that there was any chance of putting it back together again.

The surprising thing was, he wasn't sure any longer that he did want to put it back together. He had been so careful all these years to avoid any meaningful contact with other humans, so intent on his art and his drinking, that he had forgotten what it was like to live.

And now here he was in the middle of a drama unlike any he had expected, with not just one but two mysteries to solve. There was the unknown woman in Lorenzo Gagliardi's paintings, the intruders at the fort who had sliced open one of those paintings, and now this tunnel beneath the university grounds.

Noah stopped pacing. Wait a sec. That was three mysteries, not two.

He shook his head and started pacing again. However many mysteries he was embroiled in right now, it seemed that Jessica Matthews was at the heart of them. And yes, she had been like a bomb exploding in his life, but he was glad. So why was he pacing up and down in his office when he could be down there with her? Why had he even let her go down on her own? He pushed his way to the front of the group peering into the stone shaft dropping deep underground.

'Noah, what are you doing?' Professor Bianchi said.

'I'm going down there too,' he replied. 'I can't believe we all let her persuade us that she should go exploring on her own.'

'But there is no other safety harness,' Alessandro said. 'It is too dangerous.'

Noah paused, stumped for a second

by the argument he had used only an hour ago on Jessica. 'Have you got a second harness?' he asked the American student.

He shook his head. 'Sorry.'

'I'm going down anyway,' Noah said.

'Absolutely not,' Alessandro said. 'I will not permit it.'

Just then they heard a scream echoing up from the shaft.

'Jessica?' Noah shouted.

Nothing.

He looked at Alessandro. 'You can't stop me,' he said.

Alessandro nodded grimly. Noah slipped over the edge and started climbing down into the darkness.

11

The tunnel was small, but not too tight to fit through. Jessica was able to crawl along on her hands and knees still. The ground here was dry rock, and Jessica wondered if the well had only filled up with water to the point where there was now mud.

She had never heard of a tunnel at the bottom of a well before. This had to be some sort of secret tunnel, designed when the abbey was originally built to house something. Whatever it was, the monks had gone to a lot of trouble to make sure no one ever found it.

A tunnel at the bottom of a well. The well capped off with a trapdoor, opened with a key that worked the opposite to how it should. And the key hidden in the statuette of Julian the Hospitaller.

Jessica stopped shuffling along for a moment. Hadn't Noah mentioned something about the monks being entrusted with protecting the sword that Julian had used to smite his enemy? The same sword he had used unwittingly on his mother and father?

And what about the gold and silver? In Noah's retelling of the legend, he had said that Julian had given away much of his wealth, using it to build hospitals and houses for the poor. But what if there had been gold left? Wouldn't the monks have been entrusted with protecting that, too? Or maybe they would have just spent it.

Jessica continued crawling, her head torch picking out stark shadows in the rough-hewn rock walls. Occasionally her helmet bumped against the low roof, or scraped along a ridge of rock. She was just thankful she wasn't claustrophobic.

The tunnel was beginning to feel like it was never going to end. Jessica began to wonder how long she should keep shuffling along; that maybe she should think about turning back at some point.

It suddenly occurred to her that she couldn't actually turn around; that the tunnel was too narrow.

Jessica stopped crawling again. She would have to shuffle backwards all the way to the opening at the bottom of the well!

Well, it was your stupid idea to come down here! You had to be the one to go exploring, didn't you? You should have called in the experts and let them come down here — people who know what they're doing!

That was Harrison talking. Despite being free of him, Jessica still found that sometimes his hectoring voice would penetrate her mind and scold her over something. 'Go away, Harrison,' she muttered.

Still, she had to make a decision now. Call it a day and start the painfully slow job of shuffling all the way back to the start of the tunnel, with her bottom leading the way? Or explore a little further in the hope that the tunnel widened out at some point, giving her enough space to turn around?

There was no contest, really. Until she married Harrison and began turning into a boring, submissive housewife, Jessica had never been one for turning back. Life had always seemed just too exciting and full of possibilities for that.

And now here she was again, exploring, investigating, experiencing what life had to give her. Yes, Harrison was still there in the back of her mind, scolding her, telling her to stop being so silly and start acting like a grown-up. But his voice was growing fainter by the day. And here was another opportunity to extinguish it even further.

Jessica began shuffling forward again. The light from her torch picked out a shadow up ahead. Was that an opening in the side of the tunnel?

She picked up her pace, eager for a change of scenery at least. Despite not suffering from claustrophobia, she was starting to feel that the tunnel walls were closing in on her a little more. She had to keep control of herself. The last thing she needed right now was to start having a panic attack.

Jessica was aware that the palms of her hands were starting to sting, and her knees ache, from the constant crawling over the hard rock. She would be glad for the chance to turn around and head back, to get out of here. There was a definite gap in the side of the tunnel, which was good, as she could now see that up ahead was simply a dead end. At least if the gap in the side was only shallow, it would still give her room to turn around so that she could head back.

Jessica finally reached the end of the tunnel. It was only later, after the shock had worn off of seeing that other thing, that she would properly notice the locked heavy wooden door set into the rocky wall.

But it was the crumpled skeleton, the skull staring at her, that she saw first.

And that made her scream.

'I don't know what came over me,' Jessica said.

'You're underground in an enclosed space and you just stumbled across a skeleton,' Noah remarked. 'I think you're excused a scream. I think most people would have reacted the same way.'

They were huddled together in the darkness, looking at the remains of the skeleton, at its pale white bones and the grinning skull. Jessica shuddered. She was glad to have Noah with her.

He had kept calling her name as he descended the stone shaft until she answered. Then, as he had crawled along the tunnel, he had kept talking to her, keeping up a constant stream of reassurances until, finally, she told him to stop.

'I'm fine,' she'd said. 'Really, I'm all right.'

Noah had called up to the others that Jessica was fine, that she had just been spooked a little. But he didn't say what by. Now they were huddled together, looking at the skeleton lying in front of the heavy oak door.

'Who do you think he was?' Noah said.

'And how long has he been down here?' Jessica replied.

Noah reached out and placed a hand against the door. 'And what on earth is behind here?'

'Now we have another lost key to start looking for,' Jessica said. 'Are there any more precious artefacts in the museum that my mother could smash?'

Noah grinned. 'I'm sure we could find her something. Looks like we're going to have to get a locksmith down here to get this thing opened up. Preferably one who isn't claustrophobic and doesn't scream at the sight of skeletons.'

Punching him lightly on the arm, Jessica said, 'I bet you'd have done the same if you had stumbled across that thing on your own down here.'

Noah rubbed at his arm in a mock show of pain. 'More than likely I would.'

'Hey, wait a minute! What about the other statuette of Julian in the crypt? Maybe that has the second key inside it!'

Noah grinned. 'I hadn't thought of that.' His smile faded.

'What?'

'I'm just not sure how keen Alessandro will be at the thought of smashing into pieces another precious ancient artefact.'

'I see what you mean. But how else are we going to find out if there's a key inside it?'

'I don't know. Maybe an X-ray?'

'Maybe.' Jessica paused thoughtfully. 'You know, that really was very gallant of you to come racing down here and rescue me.'

Noah grinned. 'All in a day's work. Just part of being the resident artist at the University of Trento.'

'This happens lots, does it?'

'Didn't you realise? Practically every day I have to rescue a damsel in distress. It's just fortunate I didn't have to ride Ernie down here. He doesn't like enclosed spaces.'

Jessica burst out laughing. 'Who's Ernie?'

'My white stallion,' Noah said. 'Surely you must know that all knights in shining armour have a white stallion.'

Before she knew what she was doing, before she was aware even of the rush of desire overpowering her, Jessica lunged forward and pulled Noah to her. Their lips met, his hands in her hair, her hands around his back. The enclosed space of the tunnel, the darkness, the grisly discovery and the locked door, all of it disappeared beneath Noah's touch.

He ran his hands through her hair and she pulled him closer, tighter against her, as the kiss went on and on. Everything was forgotten. Her mother, Professor Bianchi and the others waiting up in Noah's office, the mystery that she had come to Italy to solve. All of it gone in the heat of Noah's embrace, in the passion of his kiss.

Suddenly he pulled back. 'I'm sorry,' he said, lowering his head. 'I shouldn't have — '

'It wasn't you, it was me,' Jessica whispered, placing a hand under his chin and tilting his head up to face hers.

'Jessica, I — '

She cut short his words by planting her mouth on his once more. For a moment she thought he might pull away again, and the passion and the heat running through her body would dissolve, leaving her cold and sad. But no, he returned her kiss with a force and desperation she hadn't expected. She welcomed it, threw herself into it, allowed it to swallow her up. Nothing else mattered right now; they could have been anywhere in the world and she wouldn't have noticed. All that mattered was Noah and his embrace, his kiss.

Jessica became vaguely aware of a voice calling to them, echoing down the tunnel. 'Jessica? Jessica! Are you there, are you all right?'

She pulled away from Noah, breathless. 'We're all right, Mum!' she shouted. 'Everything's fine!' *Everything is more than fine*, she thought.

Noah pushed his long hair back off his face and leaned his back against the wall. 'Wow, you certainly know how to kiss!' he whispered.

'You're not too bad yourself,' Jessica murmured, grinning.

He wiped a hand across his eyes. She placed a gentle hand on his shoulder. 'Are you crying?' she said. With only the light from their torches, and the shadows flickering all around, it was hard for her to see Noah properly.

'My eyes might be leaking a little, yes,' he replied.

Jessica leaned over and wrapped her arms around him, hugging him tight. 'But why? What's wrong?' she whispered, although she thought she could guess.

'I haven't felt this way about someone else for so long now,' he said, his voice muffled against her shoulder. 'Not for years, not since I lost Sarah.'

'Alessandro told me about the accident,' Jessica whispered. 'I'm so sorry for you. It must have hurt so much.'

Noah gripped her tighter. 'It did, and it still does. And I locked myself away, buried myself in my work, and the drink, believing that I could make it all disappear. That I could use these things to build a protective wall around myself and never allow myself to feel that way about anyone again.' He paused and took a deep breath. 'And then you came along and ruined it all.'

Jessica giggled. 'I'll take that as a compliment.'

Noah lifted his head off her shoulder and looked into her eyes. 'Yes, please do.'

They kissed again, more gently this

time, but still losing themselves in each other.

'Jessica! What's going on down there?'

Jessica pulled away and rolled her eyes. 'Oh, Mother!'

'I heard that! What are you doing down there?'

Jessica's eyes widened with shock and Noah buried his face in his hands as he attempted to stifle snorts of laughter.

'How much do you think they can hear up there?' she whispered.

Noah was too busy struggling to hold back fits of laughter to answer.

Jessica started giggling too, until she happened to see the skeleton lying beside Noah, its empty eye sockets gazing up at her. The laughter died on her lips. 'We'll be up in a minute!' she shouted, and tugged on Noah's sleeve.

He looked where she was pointing and his laughter faded too. 'Hey, I'd forgotten all about him,' he whispered.

'Or her,' Jessica said.

Noah leaned forward and took a

closer look at the skull. 'I wonder how long he or she has been down here.'

Jessica shuddered. 'I'm not sure I even want to think about that.'

He sighed. 'And that's my peace and quiet completely disrupted for the next few weeks, or even months.'

'Why, what do you mean?'

'Because every archaeologist, palae-ontologist and probably every other ologist you can think of will descend upon my office to take a look down here at this poor fella. He's not going to get much peace either.'

'Do you think he'll mind?'

'Probably not.' Noah looked up at the locked heavy wooden door. 'And everyone's going to be wondering what on earth is behind that door, too.'

'We found the key inside the statuette of Julian,' Jessica said. 'Do you think it might be his gold and silver, hidden here for safekeeping?'

'Could be,' Noah mused. 'Truth is, it's just as likely to be the Wizard of Oz or Blackbeard's treasure. The worrying thing is, everybody else is going to be thinking the same as you, and so we can add treasure hunters to the list of ologists who will be disturbing my peace from this point on.'

'That would make them treasure hunterologists,' Jessica said. 'I don't think it has much of a ring to it really.'

'I don't care what they call themselves, just as long as they keep out of my way.'

'Noah! Jessica!' This time it was Alessandro's voice that echoed down the rocky tunnel.

'We're on our way out!' Noah shouted.

Jessica took one last look at the heavy oak door set in the stone wall. So many mysteries.

What an exciting trip this had turned out to be.

In more ways than one.

* * *

The time it took to crawl back through the tunnel and climb up the well shaft into Noah's office went a lot faster than Jessica's journey into the depths of the underworld. And that was how it felt to her — like she had visited a subterranean world far removed from her normal existence. Everyone crowded around them as they emerged from the square hole in the office floor. And they all started talking at once.

What did you find down there?

Why did you scream?

Where does the tunnel lead?

What took you so long?

This last question was from Jessica's mother. And from the look on her face, it seemed she already had her own idea of the answer to that question.

In the end, Professor Bianchi took control and raised his voice to shout, 'Please! Everyone, be quiet!'

The voices quickly died down until there was silence.

'Thank you,' Alessandro said. 'Now, Jessica and Noah have had a traumatic experience, and we must give them a chance to rest. And I know you are all eager to go down and take a look at this skeleton for yourselves, as am I; but we must not. In fact, I suppose we must now treat it as a crime scene and not disturb it until the *polizia* have been.'

'*Una scena del crimine?*' someone said.

'*Sì, è giusto,*' Professor Bianchi replied. 'Until the *polizia* allow us access, we must stay away. *Nessuno è permesso laggiù, capisci?*'

Everyone reluctantly murmured their agreement. With the excitement having dissipated somewhat, people began slowly filing out of Noah's office.

When the last of the students and staff had left, Angela placed her hands on her hips and stared at Jessica and Noah. 'Right, then — now that we're on our own, you can tell us what really happened down there,' she said.

'What do you mean?' Jessica said, glancing at Noah.

Professor Bianchi suddenly found something of extreme interest to look at out of Noah's window.

'I mean, what took the two of you so long?' Angela said. 'And don't try and tell me you were sitting there looking at a dead body all that time, because I don't believe you.'

'But that's exactly what we were doing,' Jessica replied, her chest growing tight with indignation.

'And is that why Noah's suddenly wearing lipstick?' Angela said, unable to hide a smile as she spoke.

Noah quickly wiped the back of his hand across his mouth. Jessica's face flushed with heat.

'Never mind,' Angela said, her tone softer now. 'I suppose it's none of my business.'

Jessica glanced at Noah, afraid that he might be angry, or that his instincts to run and hide might have kicked in. He was looking back at her from beneath a floppy fringe of hair.

And he was smiling.

12

'We should enjoy the peace and quiet while it lasts,' Noah said after Alessandro and Angela had left. 'It's not going to last long, I can promise you.'

Professor Bianchi had offered to take Jessica and her mother back up to Stefania's house in his car, but Jessica had said she wanted to stay back at the university a little while longer.

'Come along, Alessandro, let's leave these two lovebirds alone,' Angela had said.

Now that they were on their own, the silence and emptiness of the office suddenly seemed awkward. Had the kiss they had shared underground been more of a product of the moment than anything else?

But then Noah took Jessica in a gentle embrace, washing away the awkwardness she had suddenly felt. She lay her head against his chest as she wrapped her arms around him. 'Are you really all right with me forcing myself on you down there?' she said.

'I'm more than all right with it,' Noah replied. 'I've been besotted with you since the first moment I laid eyes on you.'

Jessica pulled back and looked up at him. 'Seriously? You did nothing but insult me!'

'Ouch. I know — don't remind me.'

'That's all right. You've made up for it since,' Jessica said, laying her head against his chest again.

'You were attacking my defences,' Noah continued. 'All these years I'd spent carefully building walls between myself and the outside world, and any meaningful connections with other people; and then you came along, and within minutes the walls were crumbling and the towers were falling. I was scared.'

'There's no need to be scared.'

'Since I lost Sarah, I've been terrified

of forming another relationship with someone else, only to lose them too. I couldn't go through that again.'

'You won't have to. I'm not going anywhere.'

Noah squeezed her tighter. Jessica lifted her face to his, and their lips met. She swept her fingers through his hair as they kissed, a heat rising from the pit of her stomach and across her chest. Finally, reluctantly, they parted.

Noah looked at his watch and groaned. 'Oh no, I've got a lecture in five minutes! I need to get out of here.'

Suddenly he was running around his office, grabbing at books and sheaves of paper, seemingly at random. 'I'll see you later,' he said, giving Jessica a quick peck on the lips and then opening the office door.

'Wait!' she said.

Noah paused, an eyebrow raised.

Jessica pointed at her lips.

Noah grinned, pulled some tissue from a pocket, and wiped Jessica's lipstick off his mouth.

* * *

With nothing left to do, but her head spinning with the events of the last couple of hours, Jessica decided to head down to the caféteria and grab herself a drink. She thought she might even go and sit in the abbey ruins for a little while and absorb the peacefulness and the quiet. All of a sudden, it seemed she had a lot to be thinking about.

Looking at the open trapdoor, she thought it might be a good idea to lock it. Whilst the office was empty, some enterprising and curious student might get it into his or her head to go exploring.

Jessica pulled the heavy trapdoor closed, and it fell shut with a dull thud. She used the key to lock it and absently slipped it into a pocket.

As she walked to the café, Jessica's thoughts turned back to Lorenzo Gagliardi and the painting of the mysterious young woman. In all the excitement of finding and opening the trapdoor leading underground to a second, even more mysterious door, not to mention her passionate clinch with Noah, she had forgotten all about her original reason for coming to Italy. This trip was turning out to be a lot more exciting than she had anticipated.

The café was quiet, and Jessica was easily able to find a table to herself. She sat and nursed a coffee, her mind whirling with thoughts of Gagliardi's paintings, grinning skulls, Nazi insignia, underground rooms, and Noah.

Most of all, Noah.

Jessica had most definitely not come to Trento looking for romance, but it seemed romance had found her. But she was only here for another week. What would happen when she returned to England? Say goodbye and put the experience down as a holiday fling? Try a long-distance relationship, mainly involving communicating by Skype and email?

She frowned. That was no good. Internet technology was amazing, and growing even more amazing by the day it seemed, but as far as she knew no one had yet invented a way of kissing via video conferencing. And even if someone did invent that tomorrow, it still sounded very unappealing.

Her coffee was still too hot to comfortably drink, but Jessica took a sip anyway. It was a way of distracting herself, breaking up her thoughts. As one thought blossomed in her mind, another pushed it out of the way.

If only Noah hadn't had to go to his lecture, they could have sat down and talked about everything. About the paintings, about the underground locked room, about the skeleton. But most importantly, they could have talked about themselves and their burgeoning relationship.

'Excuse me. I hope you don't mind the intrusion, but may I join you?'

Jessica glanced up, startled. The old man, William, stood by her table, a cup of tea in his hand.

'Why, yes of course!' Jessica replied,

her thoughts scattering.

William sat down and placed his cup of tea on the table. 'Are you sure you don't mind?' he asked. 'It just seems such a shame for the two of us to be sitting on our own when we've already met.'

'I don't mind at all,' Jessica said. 'How was your meeting with Noah?'

'Mr Glassman?' William took a sip of his tea. 'Oh, it was most interesting. Mr Glassman obviously has a deep interest in Lorenzo Gagliardi's work, and knows a great deal about him.'

'So the meeting was helpful?'

'I'm afraid not, no.' He took another sip of his tea. 'I'm afraid he had nothing new to tell me that I didn't already know about Lorenzo and his work.'

'Oh dear, I'm sorry.'

'Not at all, my dear. Being able to share some time with a pretty young lady has more than made up for my lack of success.'

Jessica smiled. 'You're very sweet. But what do you mean, lack of success?

Is there something specific you're searching for?'

'Of course there is. The same thing that you are looking for, and no doubt many others. The solution to the mystery of the young woman's identity in his final paintings.'

'I get the feeling that is going to remain a mystery for a very long time to come, possibly forever.'

'You may be correct there. It seems you've had quite an exciting morning here. I heard talk of a tunnel being discovered beneath the university.'

'Yes, and the entrance is in Noah's office, of all places.'

'And someone went down and found a dead body down there?'

Jessica laughed. 'It was more of a skeleton than a dead body. A very old skeleton, from the looks of it. And yes, that person who so foolishly climbed down into the tunnel beneath the university is me.'

William's bushy eyebrows rose on his forehead. 'Well I never. You're a very brave young woman, as well as being so pretty.'

If you weren't ninety-five years old, I'd swear you were flirting with me, Jessica thought. *Who knows, maybe you are.* 'I don't know about brave. Impetuous, maybe.'

'Did you find anything else besides a skeleton?' William asked. He had leaned forward in his chair as he spoke, and there was a look of eagerness on his lined face.

'A door,' Jessica said. 'There was a locked door — a square heavy-looking wooden door.'

William leaned back in his chair and sighed.

'Is everything all right?' she asked.

He pulled a white silk handkerchief from his pocket and wiped his forehead. 'Yes, I'm fine, thank you. When you get to my age, you'll find that sometimes you have flushes and moments of feeling a little faint.'

Jessica glanced around the café, wondering if she should get help. But when she looked back at William, he seemed fine again.

'I suppose the experts will be arriving in the next few days, and ruin everything,' William said.

'Ruin everything? What do you mean?'

He leaned forward again. 'That's what they do in their quest to discover, to excavate, to take apart and then attempt to reconstruct. The answer is already staring them in the face, if only they could see it.'

'I'm not sure I follow.'

William lifted his hand in apology. 'I'm so sorry. Do excuse the ramblings of an old man. I've lived so long, it seems I'm out of my time now; that I belong in the past, with Lorenzo and his paintings.'

'Don't say things like that.'

He waved her protests away. 'Anyway, I must be going.' He finished drinking his tea. 'Tell me, before I go, does anyone have a key for this locked door deep beneath the university?'

'Not that we know of,' Jessica said. 'The only key we have is the one for the trapdoor in Noah's office.' She pulled the key from her pocket and laid it on the table. 'And the funny thing is, you have to put the handle end in the lock to open the trapdoor.'

'That's unusual, and ingenious,' William said, looking at the key. 'Well, I really must go.' He looked at her and smiled. 'I do hope we see each other again.'

'Thank you. So do I.' She pocketed the key and watched him leave. He walked briskly.

He really is amazing for his age, she thought. *But he is a little strange.*

* * *

Jessica decided to head back to Stefania's house. After the events of the last few hours, her head still spinning with everything that had happened, she needed a lie-down, maybe even a nap. She caught a bus up the steep winding road and gazed out of the window at the mountains topped with snow in the distance. The view calmed her somewhat, and when she alighted at her stop she was already starting to feel a little calmer.

The feeling didn't last.

A police car was parked outside Stefania's house. Two *polizia* were climbing into the car as Jessica approached. They regarded her coolly as they drove away.

'Stefania!' she called as she entered the house. 'Is everything all right?'

Jessica stopped in her tracks at the sight that met her. The contents of the living room looked as though they had been picked up by a tornado as it swept through the house and tore everything apart.

Stefania appeared in the kitchen doorway, her face ashen. Tomasso stood beside her, clutching her hand. He saw Jessica, but there was no usual greeting of, 'Hey you! You wanna fight?' Instead he turned and ran into his bedroom.

'Oh, Stefania,' Jessica said. 'What happened?'

'When we came home, this is how we found the house,' Stefania said.

Caterina appeared behind her mother, too. 'They stole my sketchbook,' she said, and a tear began rolling down her cheek.

A picture of Cora and Willem entered Jessica's mind. She could see them turning over everything inside the house, searching for Caterina's sketchbook, with the drawings of Gagliardi's paintings in it. But why? What possible use could they have for a teenager's drawings of a series of paintings? Did they seriously think that Caterina held the answer to the mystery of Gagliardi's recently discovered late-period work? And just why was the answer so important to them?

'Oh, Caterina, I'm so sorry,' Jessica said. 'I feel like this is all my fault.'

'No,' Stefania said. 'This is not your fault at all. These people, whoever they

234

are, are criminals. They are the ones at fault, not you.'

'But it's because of me, I'm sure, that they broke into your lovely home and stole Caterina's sketchpad.'

Jessica felt close to tears herself. She had no clue at all as to what might be going on, but she knew that she had brought unhappiness into the lives of these people who had welcomed her into their home and shown her such love.

'Don't be silly,' Stefania said, and motioned to Jessica as she crossed the room towards her.

Stefania enveloped Jessica in a hug. Unable to hold back the tears anymore, Jessica began crying softly as she felt Caterina's arms embracing her too.

This is so silly! These lovely people are the ones who have had their home violated, and yet they're the ones comforting me!

Jessica suddenly realised another pair of arms was hugging her. She looked down at Tomasso gazing back up at her, his arms around her.

And that was it. The tears became a flood.

★　★　★

Noah finished his lectures and headed back to his office. It had been a tiring day, and the temptation was there to lock himself in and crack open a bottle of whisky. But he knew he wouldn't, not today. Noah wasn't suffering from alcoholism. But he knew he had been heading that way for sure, before Jessica erupted into his life and destroyed all his defences.

The temptation was there to drink; but his days of drinking on his own, hidden away from humanity, were over. Although they hadn't arranged anything, Noah was sure he would be seeing Jessica later on. He could have a drink then, and share a glass of wine with her, while they discussed everything that had happened today.

It was funny, but since unburdening

himself to Jessica about losing Sarah, it seemed as though he had managed to shrug off a huge backpack that had been weighing him down all these years. Almost as though he was light enough to fly. He smiled at the thought. How things had changed in just the matter of a few days.

Opening his office door, he stepped inside and pulled up short in surprise. 'What on earth are you doing here?' he snapped.

Cora was sitting on his desk, one foot on the floor and the other on the desktop, an arm draped over her knee.

'Really,' she said, 'is that any way to greet an old friend?'

Noah closed the door softly behind him. He had a sudden irrational fear that someone might come along and see her. And for some reason he couldn't pin down, that thought unsettled him deeply. 'Is that what we are? Old friends?'

'We were more than friends once,' Cora replied as she stood up, slowly, languidly.

'That was a long time ago. There have been a lot of changes since then, especially for you, it looks like.'

She drew closer, a small smile hovering on her black lips. 'What's the matter, Noah? Don't you like my appearance? Do I unsettle you?'

Noah had to fight the urge to back up, to fling open his office door and flee. 'You always unsettled me a little, Cora, even back during that brief time when we were an item.'

The tip of Cora's tongue snaked out and licked her top lip before disappearing again. 'Did you know I've never been with another man since we split up?'

Noah laughed. 'I don't believe that for a moment! And we didn't split up, I dumped you.'

Cora pouted. 'You can be so cruel sometimes.'

Noah couldn't help but notice that she was wearing a pair of figure-hugging black trousers and a black T-shirt that looked so tight on her torso it could have been spray-painted on. Was this all for his benefit? Was she attempting to seduce him?

'What do you want, Cora?' Noah said. 'Just tell me, and then get out. Or, preferably, just skip the part where you tell me what you want, and just go straight to the part where you leave.'

Cora stood up a little straighter, visibly dropping the sexy little girl act. Inwardly, Noah breathed a sigh of relief. As she moved, her T-shirt shifted, one of the sleeves sliding a little higher, revealing a tattoo on her upper arm. Noah grabbed at her T-shirt, pulling the sleeve back.

'A swastika!' he gasped.

Cora pulled away from him, grabbed the edge of her T-shirt sleeve and pulled it back down again, covering the tattoo.

'What's going on, Cora?' Noah demanded. 'Have you got yourself mixed up with a neo-Nazi group now? Think you and your brother are part of the superior race, is that it? I always knew you had some far-out ideas, but this — ?' He shook his head in disgust.

'You're so stupid,' Cora hissed. 'You think you know it all. You think you're the superior one, you and that little floozy of yours. But you don't know *anything*!'

'Was it you?' Noah said. 'Did you and that brother of yours ransack my office? Paint all those crude, nasty symbols on my walls?'

'And what if it was?'

'What were you looking for?'

Cora smirked. 'Nothing. I just wanted to pay you a visit and leave a little reminder behind, something you wouldn't ever forget.'

'I don't believe you,' Noah snapped. 'The graffiti was a cover, a distraction from the fact that you were searching for something. What is it, Cora? What are you doing here in Trento?'

She said nothing, but her eyes flicked towards the trapdoor set in the floor.

'What's that to you?' Noah said. 'And what's the connection between that and your visits to the Gagliardi exhibition?

And that night at the fortress, you and Willem were the intruders, weren't you? You broke into the museum to slash Gagliardi's paintings. But why?'

Again, Cora said nothing.

'There's a connection, isn't there? Something you know that the rest of us don't. A larger mystery. But you haven't got all the pieces either, have you? Otherwise, why would you be here?'

Cora suddenly pushed past him, reaching for the door handle. He grabbed her arm, but she twisted away and stuck her face in his, her features contorted into a snarl.

'Get off me! You'll find out soon enough!' And with that she was gone, slamming the door behind her.

Noah breathed a sigh of relief. He felt shaky inside, as though he had been in danger and was now safe again.

Cora had always been a little strange, out of kilter with the rest of society. But now she seemed positively deranged. What did she mean, *You'll find out soon enough?* As though she had something big planned, her and that crazy violent brother of hers.

'The mystery deepens,' Noah muttered, gazing at the trapdoor set in the office floor. He thought of the locked heavy oak door set in the rock face deep underground, guarded by a skeleton. What could be behind that door that fascinated Cora so much? And what did that have to do with the paintings?

Gagliardi. Everything pointed back to Lorenzo Gagliardi. Only that wasn't quite right, was it?

The unknown woman in Gagliardi's paintings. She was the focus of this mystery.

13

They all sat around the large coffee table in Stefania's lounge, mulling over the incidents of the last few days. Fabrizio made everyone drinks and joined them. No one spoke for a while, and even Tomasso was not his usual live-wire self.

'You really have got yourself in a pickle this time,' Angela said, finally breaking the silence, directing her comment at Jessica.

'What do you mean by that?' Jessica retorted, indignation rising in her chest.

'Well, here you are, supposedly in Italy for a relaxing break looking at some dusty old paintings, and now you've got yourself mixed up in some Nazi plot! It's like something out of an Alfred Hitchcock film!'

'You're the one who's always telling

me to have some excitement in my life,' Jessica replied.

'I didn't mean this much excitement.'

'I still think you should call the *polizia*,' Stefania said.

'And tell them what?' Noah asked. 'That an ex-girlfriend of mine draped herself over my desk in a hideous attempt at flirting with me and told me something was going to happen? About the only crime I can think of that I can prove she has committed is her awful fashion sense.'

'What about the swastika tattoo on her arm?' Jessica said. 'Isn't that some kind of hate crime?'

Noah took a sip of his coffee. 'I don't know. Even if it is, what are the police going to do? Arrest her and order her to have it removed? Maybe they could employ a tattoo artist who could ink a pretty flower over the top of it, or fluffy bunny rabbits and a unicorn.'

Caterina snorted with laughter. She was sitting cross-legged in a chair with a new sketchpad, and she was busy drawing.

Jessica sighed. 'I really don't understand what the connection could be between the tunnel underneath your office and Lorenzo Gagliardi's paintings.'

'Don't forget the skeleton,' Noah said.

'And the locked room,' Stefania said. 'I really want to know what's behind that door.'

'Alessandro has arranged for a locksmith to come out tomorrow and have a go at opening the lock,' Noah said. 'There's also a team of archaeologists on their way.'

'Any treasure-hunterologists?' Jessica asked.

Noah rolled his eyes. 'Probably.'

Caterina looked up from her sketchpad. 'What's a treasure-hunterologist?'

'It's a made-up word,' Jessica said, smiling. 'It's a term invented by Noah, and refers to anyone who dares disturb Noah Glassman in his office.' Jessica craned her head to look at Caterina's sketchpad. 'What are you drawing?'

'Lorenzo Gagliardi's lady friend.' Caterina held out her pad for everyone to see.

'Wow!' Jessica gasped. 'Caterina, that's amazing. You're so good at drawing, and you have a fantastic memory!'

Caterina smiled and blushed a little.

'May I?' Noah asked. He reached out and took the pad off Caterina.

Jessica studied the sketch with him. Caterina's sketch was of one of her favourites from the paintings she had seen, and she had managed to capture Gagliardi's style in that particular one. Even more, though, she had managed to recreate Gagliardi's subject, right down to the fierce expression of determination on her face and the clenched fist at her side.

'Caterina has always been good at drawing,' Fabrizio said.

'She's not *good* at drawing, she's *amazing*,' Noah replied. 'Have you got any other drawings here? I'd love to see them.'

Caterina beamed and stood up. 'I've got lots. I'll go and get some.'

Noah put the sketchpad on the sofa next to Tomasso as Caterina hurried out of the living room.

Stefania chuckled. 'I'm afraid that's your evening taken over. Caterina loves to show off her artistic skills.'

'I'm quite happy with that,' Noah replied. 'Honestly, based on that one sketch alone, I think she could get a place at the university.'

'When she's older, you mean?' Fabrizio said.

'No, I mean now!'

'You think she is that good?' Stefania said.

'I certainly do. She's a very talented young woman.'

Fabrizio and Stefania looked at each other and smiled. Fabrizio stood up. 'Would anyone like another drink?'

'Now, I'm not meaning to be rude or anything,' Angela said, 'but isn't it about time we stopped drinking all this coffee and tea and opened a bottle of wine?'

'Mother!' Jessica groaned.

'Don't you 'mother' me,' Angela said.

Fabrizio laughed. 'I was just about to suggest that very thing.'

Jessica received a look from her mother that seemed to say, *I told you so.*

As Fabrizio left the room, Caterina returned, her arms filled with sketch-pads and sheets of drawings and paintings. Her look of happiness suddenly turned to one of thunder. 'Tomasso!' she shrieked.

Tomasso dropped Caterina's sketch-pad and pencil that he had been holding, as though it had suddenly grown red-hot.

'Oh, Tomasso!' Stefania said. '*Perchè lo hai fatto? Hai rovinato il disegno di Caterina!*'

'*Mi dispiace, mamma, non volevo!*' Tomasso cried, looking close to tears.

'What's wrong?' Jessica asked.

Stefania shook her head in frustration. 'It's Tomasso. He gets the devil in him sometimes. He's drawn all over Caterina's sketch.'

Noah picked up the sketchpad again to look at what Tomasso had done. His eyes widened and his mouth dropped open as he gazed at the drawing. 'I don't believe it,' he gasped, and looked up at the little boy. 'Tomasso, you're a genius!'

'What?' Jessica said, a prickle of excitement forming in her stomach.

'Wait a moment,' Noah said, and took the pencil from the space beside Tomasso. 'Caterina, may I add one more embellishment to your drawing, please?'

Caterina nodded, her face scrunched up in puzzlement.

Noah quickly sketched something over the top of Caterina's drawing. He turned the sketchpad around and held it up for everyone to see.

Jessica gasped.

★　★　★

They all gathered around a large coffee-table-sized book of history and stared at the photograph. It had been Jessica's idea to ask Stefania if they had a book of local history, as she had noticed every room in their house contained bookshelves stacked high with books. Noah laid Caterina's sketch down on the book, beside the photograph.

'Well, there certainly does seem to be a resemblance,' Angela said.

'There's more than just a resemblance,' Noah replied. 'It's the same person.'

'There was always something that bothered me about those paintings, but I could never pin it down,' Jessica said. 'Now I know what it was. Gagliardi's young woman just looked too masculine.'

Over the top of Caterina's sketch, Tomasso had drawn a moustache on the face of the mysterious woman. Noah had added a sword, placing the hilt in her fist at her waist, the blade arching up beside her. The effect had been astonishing, immediately transforming the mysterious young woman into Julian the Hospitaller. Laying the drawing by the side of an illustration of Julian in Caterina's history book had confirmed it.

'But what does it mean?' Angela said.

Fabrizio stood up and said, 'I think it means we should have another drink! I never did give you that glass of wine, Angela.' He went to the kitchen to open the bottle of wine. Everybody else returned to their seats.

Jessica looked at Noah. He ran a hand through his long hair, pushing it off his face. She had a sudden urge to ask Caterina if she had any hairdressing scissors. Although it had been a long time since she had cut anyone's hair, she was sure she still had the knack. She imagined herself standing behind him, combing his hair, trimming it, their bodies close. *You mustn't even suggest it*, she thought. *You'll only end up scaring him off if you do.* She brought her attention back to the present moment.

'I don't know if this explains the mystery of Gagliardi's paintings or deepens it,' Noah was saying.

'Why would he have painted all these portraits of Julian?' Jessica asked.

'Well, if you remember, before he became an artist he was a monk at the abbey.'

Jessica sat up a little straighter. 'That's right. And the abbey monks were charged with the responsibility of keeping and protecting Julian's sword after he died.'

'And where is the sword?' Stefania said.

'Nobody knows,' Noah replied. 'The legend of Julian the Hospitaller is just that, a legend. Like King Arthur and Robin Hood, his story may have been based around a kernel of truth, but nothing more.'

'What was so important about this sword?' Caterina asked.

'Would you like to tell them the

legend of Julian, or do you want me to?' Noah said, looking at Jessica.

'Let's see if I can remember it,' she said.

With only a few minor corrections from Noah, Jessica told the others the story of the hex on Julian as a newborn baby, that when he grew up he would slay his parents. She told them about his travels, and marrying the woman who one day took in his parents and gave them her bed. And how Julian was lied to by the enemy, and went back home and slew his parents with his sword, believing them to be his wife and another man lying in their marriage bed. And finally, when he discovered the truth, how he went and found the enemy and struck him with his sword, but the enemy disappeared and Julian's sword was imbued with a dark power.

Angela huffed when her daughter had finished. 'That's the second time I've heard that story today, and it still sounds more like a fairytale than anything else to me.'

'But if the legend has any truth in it,' Caterina said, 'and the monks of the abbey were really entrusted with the protection of Julian's sword, do you think . . . ?'

'That the sword might be behind the locked door in the tunnels beneath the university?' Jessica said. 'I've been wondering the exact same thing.'

'And maybe the skeleton outside the door was once a monk, standing guard over the sword,' Fabrizio said.

'Or rather crouching guard over the sword,' Noah said. 'You weren't down there. Not only is there no room to swing a cat, there's no room to actually stand upright.'

'And why would anybody want to guard the sword down there, where nobody would be going anyway, because only the monks knew about it?' Jessica said.

Fabrizio had left for the kitchen, and now he was returning with a second bottle of wine. Jessica hadn't realised they had finished off the first one. After he had refilled their glasses, Fabrizio sat down again.

'But does any of this tell us why Cora and Willem are so interested in the paintings?' he asked.

'I don't know,' Noah said. 'There's still too much of the story missing.'

'They sound more than a little crazy to me,' Angela said. 'I would stay well away from them if I was you.' She hiccupped and then giggled, putting a hand to her mouth in a show of false modesty.

'Mum, how much have you had to drink?' Jessica said.

'That's none of your business,' her mother replied primly.

Jessica sighed and shook her head. It was bad enough having her mother here at all, with her loose tongue and her forthright way of speaking her mind, whatever might be on it. But her mother here after a few glasses of red wine! There was no telling what she might come out with.

As if on cue, Angela looked at Noah

and said, 'You know, you really would look so much more handsome if you simply shaved off that dreadful beard and cut your hair. You look like a cross between a woolly mammoth and an Afghan hound.'

'Mother!' Jessica cried.

Caterina burst into a fit of giggles, and Tomasso joined her, even though he didn't understand what had been said.

'Well I'm only saying what everybody else is thinking,' Angela said.

'It's all right, I'm not offended,' Noah said, laughing himself. 'In fact, the last couple of days I've been thinking I should go get my hair cut. It's been a while, I have to admit.'

'Jessica could do it for you,' Angela said. 'She used to cut her dad's hair all the time, and her friends' too.'

'You can cut hair?' Noah asked. 'I thought you were an art student, not a hairdresser.'

Jessica blushed a little. 'I'm not a hairdresser. I just taught myself how to cut hair, that's all. Anyway, I can't cut your hair. I need some scissors, proper hairdressing scissors.'

'I've got some,' Stefania said. 'Years ago I used to have my own mobile hairdressing business. I used to cut hair at people's houses.'

'There you go,' Angela said to Noah. 'Stefania can cut your hair for you.'

Noah squirmed in his seat until Stefania came to his rescue. 'Oh no, it's years and years since I did anything like that,' she said, laughing. 'But Jessica, you can use anything that you want of mine, if you like.'

Jessica opened her mouth to say, *Oh no, thank you*, but her mother got in first.

'Oh yes, go on, Jessica. I'd love to see his handsome face behind that beard and all that hair.'

'I'm not shaving him, too!' Jessica said.

Noah raised his hand. 'Hello, everybody! I'm still here!' he said, laughing.

Stefania stood up. 'I'll go and find my

hairdressing kit.'

'I'll open another bottle of wine,' Fabrizio said, also standing up.

Caterina reached for her sketchpad and pencil. 'I'm going to draw you both while you cut his hair.'

Tomasso ran up to Jessica and raised his fists. 'Hey you! You wanna fight?'

'Oh, isn't this fun?' Angela said, draining her wine glass.

Jessica looked at Noah, a tide of panic washing through her chest. From the look on his face, he obviously felt the same way.

This is ridiculous! she thought. *They're all acting like we're a pair of performing seals! What are they going to do, sit around us in a circle and watch whilst I cut Noah's hair?*

As it turned out, Stefania took longer than expected finding her hairdressing kit. Fabrizio decided the children needed to go to bed, and Jessica's mother, deciding that she had drunk too much wine, closely followed. Left on their own in the living room, Jessica and Noah looked at each other and smiled.

'That was a close one,' Noah said.

'It certainly was,' Jessica replied. 'Honestly, sometimes my mother surprises even me with the things she comes out with.'

He chuckled. 'Don't worry about it. She doesn't mean anything.' He stood up and stretched. 'I really should be getting back.'

'Don't be silly. Sit down,' Stefania said as she came back into the living room, a large travel-type soft bag in her arms and towels on top.

'Oh, I'm afraid you're too late, everyone has gone to bed,' Noah said. 'And this performing monkey is about ready for bed too.'

Stefania smiled and put the bag down on the floor. 'No, stay a little longer. Fabrizio and I will be in the kitchen if you need anything.'

'Oh no, really — '

'Stay,' Stefania said firmly, and refilled their glasses with more wine.

'Seems our host is determined I have a haircut tonight,' Noah said when Stefania had gone.

'Yes, and she seems equally determined that I be the one to give you that haircut,' Jessica replied.

Noah took a sip of his wine. 'Well, what do you think?'

She smiled. 'I'm game if you are.'

They laid a couple of the towels on the floor in the middle of the room and placed a high stool on them. Noah sat on the stool and Jessica laid another towel across his shoulders, wrapping it gently around his throat. She opened up the bag and burst out laughing.

'Okay, why stop at a haircut? Fancy some highlights? Maybe a restyle, with curling tongs? How about a different colour altogether? Or a little more volume in your hair?'

Noah groaned. 'I'm regretting this already. If it wasn't for all that wine I've drunk, I'd be out of this place in a heartbeat.'

Jessica chose a comb and a pair of scissors.

'Are you sure you know what you're doing?' Noah said.

'Of course I do.' She sprayed his hair with water, dampening it down. Standing behind him, their bodies almost touching, she ran the comb slowly through his hair. She used her fingers to tease out the knots in it. The room was warm, and seemed to be growing warmer as Jessica continued to use the comb.

He inclined his head back a little, and it came to rest on her chest, just below her collarbone. Jessica didn't move back, just let him stay there. She slowly ran a hand down the side of his face and his neck. Felt him quiver slightly beneath her touch.

She slid her hand back up his face, her fingers through his hair. Noah reached up and took her wrist, gently pulling her hand down until he could kiss it. His lips hovered over her flesh, his breath warm in her palm. Her surroundings disappeared, all thoughts of cutting his hair gone too. She lowered her head, kissing him on the cheek, on his neck. He turned to face her, their lips touching softly. A clatter from the kitchen startled them both.

Jessica took a step back and picked up the scissors again. Took a deep breath. 'Right,' she said, her voice only a little shaky, 'how much do you want me to take off?'

'I'm completely at your mercy,' Noah said. 'Think of me as the blank canvas and you the artist. Now create a work of art.'

Jessica burst out laughing. 'No, I think I'll just give you a haircut.'

'Oh, if you insist.'

She began cutting hesitantly at first. It had been a long time since she had done this, and she didn't want to take off too much straight away. She soon settled back into the rhythm of cutting, though, and started working faster. 'I hope you're happy with this when I'm finished,' she murmured as she trimmed the hair over his ears.

'If I'm not, I'm asking for a refund,' he replied.

She stepped in front of him and leaned down with her hands on her knees so that they were face to face. 'You know what a refund of nothing is, don't you? A big fat load of nothing.'

'Is that right?' he said quietly.

They were so close their noses were almost touching. Noah leaned forward on his stool, tilting his head a little to the side. Their lips touched briefly.

'I'm supposed to be cutting your hair,' Jessica murmured.

'I know,' Noah replied, the movement of his lips caressing hers as he spoke.

Jessica pulled away and took a deep, shaky breath. 'You need to stop that. I haven't finished cutting your hair yet.'

Noah pulled a face. 'All right, then. You're the boss.'

'Too right I am, especially when I'm wielding these,' Jessica said, holding up the scissors.

She continued standing in front of

him as she worked on his hair. All of a sudden she felt self-conscious in her slim-fitting top, and how it rode up a little when she had to stretch, exposing her midriff. Noah was looking at her, she could tell that without even seeing him properly. The self-consciousness began to fade, and Jessica realised she was enjoying the experience.

'Like the view, do you?' she said.

'Very much so,' Noah murmured.

She moved around to the side, tidying up the edges of his hair. She ran her fingertips over the nape of his neck, and found herself wondering what it would feel like to let her fingers roam further, down his back and over his chest. *Pull yourself together!* she thought. *Remember where you are!*

She continued cutting, working her way around his back and to the other side until she was in front of him once more. 'There,' she said, brushing his hair with her fingers to give him a loose side parting. 'We can now safely say you no longer look like an Afghan hound.'

'That's the nicest thing you've said to me,' Noah replied. He pulled her closer to him until she was sitting on his lap. She draped an arm over his shoulders. With her other hand she pulled the towel off and let it drop to the floor.

'Not sure how I can pay you for this,' Noah murmured.

Jessica gently brushed hairs off his shirt. Her hand came to rest on his chest.

'I'm sure you'll think of something,' she whispered.

Noah leaned forward, his lips meeting hers. This time he wasn't gentle, but kissed her hard, forcefully. Jessica welcomed it and kissed him back with her own force, her own sense of urgency. She ran her fingers through his short hair, still damp. Noah bunched her long hair up in his fist, his other hand on her back pulling her closer and closer.

A giggle from the doorway startled them both. Jessica looked up just in time to see a little boyish figure running away. 'Hey you!' she hissed. 'You wanna fight?'

Noah tilted his head back and burst out laughing.

'I think we've been discovered,' Jessica said, laughing too.

'I think I need to be going home,' Noah said, still chuckling.

'Wait.' Jessica stood up and picked a mirror out of the hairdressing kit. Holding it up in front of Noah, she said, 'Is sir satisfied?'

Noah's eyes widened at the sight that met him. 'Wow, that really is a big difference.' He ran a hand over his chin. 'Now this just needs to go, and then I will no longer resemble a woolly mammoth as well as an Afghan hound.'

Jessica laughed. 'I'm so sorry about my mother!'

He stood up and pulled Jessica close. 'Don't be. And yes, to answer your original question, I'm very satisfied. Very satisfied indeed.'

And he gave her the biggest, widest smile she had ever seen.

14

'Are you all right, Alessandro?' Noah said.

The university professor appeared to be in the middle of an incipient heart attack. His eyes were as big as saucers and his mouth had formed a perfect round 'O'. He seemed incapable of speech or movement, and Noah feared he might simply keel over at any moment and hit the floor like a sack of potatoes.

'Alessandro?' Noah said again.

The professor lifted a hand and pointed a finger at him. 'You . . . you've shaved your beard, and . . . and . . . '

'Had a haircut,' Noah said, and grinned. 'Aww, you noticed. How sweet.'

'But Noah, the change, it's amazing! You look *fantastico*!'

'Hush your mouth, Professor Bianchi. You carry on like this and you'll be asking me out on a date next.'

The professor snapped his mouth shut and harrumphed. 'Does this sudden clean-up mean that you are finally rejoining the human race?'

'Now don't beat about the bush, Alessandro. Just come right out and ask me what's on your mind,' Noah said. 'And yes, I suppose it does.'

A couple of female students hurried past, giggling and talking behind their hands as they turned and glanced at Noah.

'Well I am very pleased,' Alessandro said. 'Yes, I am very pleased indeed.' And with that, the portly professor threw his arms around Noah and gave him a big hug. After a moment, he stepped back and harrumphed again. 'Now, the archaeologist specialists are arriving today to take a look at the tunnel beneath the university, and to see if they can get the locked door open without damaging it. We really do need to see what's on the other side.'

'Agreed,' Noah replied. 'Do we know

what time they're arriving?'

'Later this afternoon.'

Good, Noah thought. *That gives me some time on my own this morning.*

A couple more students walked past, male this time. 'Hey, looking good, Noah!' one of them called out.

Noah waved a hand in acknowledgement. If this was what it was going to be like today, the sooner he managed to scurry back to his office and hide, the better.

But once he got his wish and was back inside his office with the door closed behind him, the room suddenly seemed very empty. Had he really spent these last few years hiding in here, cutting himself off from humanity, as much as he could? Seemed like an awful waste of a life, all of a sudden.

He looked at his chair, the one Sarah had bought him. His last link to their life together. 'I'm sorry, Sarah,' he said. 'I never thought I'd find anyone else. I never wanted to. But, I don't know, it seems like . . . '

He couldn't say it. All of a sudden he was choked up. Last night's passionate kiss with Jessica now seemed like a betrayal of his first true love. How could he have done that?

A grey cloud of depression settled over him. Perhaps he wasn't ready to rejoin the human race just yet. He certainly wasn't ready for romance. How could he have been so foolish? He had to ring Jessica, explain that he wasn't ready, this was the wrong time. There might never be a right time.

Filled with guilt and sorrow, Noah sat down heavily in the chair. With a loud crack, it toppled over and deposited Noah on the floor. For a moment the shock of the fall stunned him into silence.

And then he started laughing.

Noah laughed until tears rolled down his cheek and his stomach started aching. Finally the laughter subsided.

'All right, Sarah,' he said softly. 'I get the message. You're dumping me, right? You've had enough of me moping around here like a sad sack. It's about time I moved on and started living again, is that what you're saying?'

As if in answer, another section of the chair snapped and fell over onto its side.

'I'll never forget you, Sarah,' Noah said, the tears coming now. 'But you're right, it's time. And I'm finally ready.'

★   ★   ★

Jessica leafed through a folder thick with pages of notes on Lorenzo Gagliardi. These notes were all of Noah's research, including the time when the painter was an unlikely prisoner of war in the Palazzo delle Albere. Something connected the artist's time there and the locked room deep beneath the foundations of the abbey. But what?

Noah had been thorough in his research, and his love of Gagliardi's work shone through the notes he had written. Jessica skimmed through the early period of Lorenzo's life, concentrating on the war years and Gagliardi's imprisonment. Unfortunately, there wasn't a huge amount of documentation of his time there. Gagliardi had been found weakened and thin through lack of proper food, his skin pale from his time spent in a dungeon.

From that point on, he had become a recluse; and, as they now knew all these years after his death, he had been producing his paintings of Julian the Hospitaller. But why? Had his time in the dungeon beneath the fortress unbalanced him mentally, perhaps taking him back to his time as a monk at the abbey, when they were all sworn to protect the sword of Julian? But how seriously had that vow been taken? Even back in the 1940s, the monks would surely have recognised what the story of Julian was — a legend, and nothing more.

The word 'legend' struck a chord in Jessica's mind, and she leafed back through Noah's notes until she found what she was looking for. There. Legend Niedermeyer, the Nazi official who made regular trips to Italy and the fortress, seemingly for the sole purpose of visiting Lorenzo Gagliardi. But what was the reason for his visits? Why was he so interested in an obscure Italian painter? Was it Niedermeyer who had ordered the German soldiers to capture Gagliardi? But again, why?

More mysteries upon mysteries. Jessica had the distinct feeling she might never find all the answers she wanted. On an impulse, she opened her laptop and Googled 'Legend Niedermeyer'. Google returned with over four hundred thousand results, but only the top two seemed relevant.

The first one was an account of a manhunt for Sturmbannführer Niedermeyer, shortly after the end of the Second World War. Despite brief sightings of him in Uruguay, Mozambique and, finally, the Dominican Republic, Niedermeyer eluded capture. The second result was a purported interview with him in 1963, in an undisclosed location in Africa. The interview was long and rambling and made little sense. Legend Niedermeyer seemed to have become even more fanatical and deluded during his time on the run, and he talked of a new world power coming soon, returning the Nazis to power and world domination.

Jessica closed down the browser in disgust, and shivered. That there had been, and still was, such evil in the world always confounded and disturbed her.

Closing the folder full of notes and putting it away, she stood at the living-room window and gazed out at the snow-topped mountains in the distance. What an unusual and exciting holiday this had turned out to be.

Now that she had stopped distracting herself with research into Gagliardi, thoughts of her passionate clinch with Noah flooded her mind. Jessica hadn't intended any of that to happen, and she was fairly sure Noah hadn't either. The embrace, that kiss, all seemed natural and unforced. Smiling, and blushing a little at the thought of how passionately Noah had kissed her, she was just grateful that Stefania or Fabrizio hadn't entered the room. She wondered what Tomasso had told his parents.

Both Stefania and Fabrizio had said nothing about last night, only asking if Noah liked his new haircut. Jessica had a feeling that they had somehow planned to leave Jessica and Noah on their own all along. And that Stefania had known where her hairdressing kit was, but had delayed bringing it back to give Jessica's mother time to grow bored and tired, and decide to go to bed. If that was the case, their plan had worked.

'Hey, you! You wanna fight?'

Jessica spun round on the spot and raised her fists at Tomasso. 'Hey, you! You wanna fight?'

Tomasso grinned and then sat on the sofa and switched on the television.

Stefania appeared in the kitchen doorway. 'I hope he didn't startle you too much.'

'Oh no, not at all!' Jessica laughed. 'I'm getting used to this young man creeping up on me.'

Tomasso grinned without turning from the television, and Jessica wondered how much he understood after all.

'Would you like another cup of tea, or coffee?' Stefania asked.

'No, I'm fine, thank you,' Jessica replied. 'In fact, I was thinking of popping into the city, and visiting the Gagliardi exhibition again.'

'Oh, can I come too?' Caterina exclaimed, sticking her head rather comically out from behind the kitchen doorway.

Jessica's heart sank a little. She had thought she might then go on to the university and see if Noah wanted to go out for lunch. All she wanted to do was spend a little time with him on her own.

Stefania seemed to sense Jessica's disappointment, and said, 'No, you must stay here and do your homework.'

'Oh, Mama!' Caterina cried. 'Please!'

'Honestly, it's no trouble,' Jessica said despite herself. 'I'd love Caterina to come with me, and I'll get her right back for her homework, I promise.'

'*Mamma, posso andare con loro?*' Tomasso shouted.

'*No, non oggi, Tomasso,*' Stefania said.

Jessica looked quizzically at Caterina, who said, 'He wants to come with us, but Mama said no.'

'Oh, I don't mind. He can come with us if he wants,' Jessica said, thinking to herself, *What am I saying?*

'Are you sure?' Stefania said. 'It would be a help to me, actually. And Caterina will look after him; he won't be any trouble.'

Jessica smiled. 'That's fine. We'll have fun, won't we, Tomasso?'

Tomasso raised his fists and said, 'Hey, you — '

'You wanna go see some paintings?' Jessica finished for him, and grinned.

★　★　★

Noah tugged at the trapdoor leading down into the tunnel beneath the university, but it refused to open. He had already known that the door would not open before he tried it, because this wasn't the first time he had attempted to pull it open. But he just couldn't help trying again.

The thing was locked, and Noah had no idea where the key was. He sat on the floor beside the ruins of his chair and stared at the trapdoor, as though willing it to magically open up all by itself.

But Noah knew that doors didn't do that. When they were locked, which this one most certainly was, they needed a key to unlock them. And Noah had already spent the morning turning his office upside down looking for one.

This is stupid, he thought. *The key*

has to be around here somewhere.

He looked at the other statuette of Julian, now sitting on his desk. He had been down to the crypt earlier that morning and taken it from its alcove. 'What about you then?' he said. 'Have you got another key inside your belly? For that second door at the end of the tunnel?'

Julian gazed silently back at Noah.

'You know what, I'm not kidding around here. You'd better tell me what you know, or I'm coming over there and breaking you in half, and then you won't be happy, will you?'

Again, Julian said nothing.

'Ah, forget it,' Noah said. 'You think you're tough, but I'm telling you now, you'll break under my questioning eventually.'

There was a knock at the office door. Noah scrambled to his feet, but slipped on a piece of the broken chair and fell back down again. The door opened.

'Ah, Noah,' Professor Alessandro

said, poking his head around inside the office. 'I hope we're, ah, not interrupting anything.'

'Not a thing,' Noah said. 'I'm just having a sit-down, that's all.'

'It's just, I thought I heard voices.'

'Yeah, that was me. I was interrogating Julian over there, but he's keeping quiet. Thinks he's a tough guy, but I'm going to show him otherwise.'

'Ah, I see,' Alessandro said, his face a picture of confusion. He entered the office, followed by a little squirrel-faced man and an even smaller woman. 'These are the archaeological experts, come to inspect the tunnel.'

Ignoring Noah, the man and woman approached the trapdoor, talking rapidly in Italian. The man bent down and pulled at the trapdoor, but it refused to budge.

'It's locked,' Noah said.

Alessandro looked at him, eyebrows raised.

Noah shrugged. 'I can't find the key anywhere.'

Alessandro imparted this information to the odd-looking pair. Without a word, they started looking for the key, rifling through Noah's drawers and opening cupboards.

Noah opened his mouth to protest and then snapped it shut again. There really didn't seem much point. Climbing to his feet, he said to Alessandro, 'I'm going to get myself a cup of coffee. Let me know when Charlie Farley and Piggy Malone here have finished ransacking my office, will you?'

★ ★ ★

The Gagliardi exhibition was busier than ever. This might have been good for the Palazzo delle Albere and for Gagliardi's reputation, but not for Jessica. She hated crowds, hated being hemmed in by people.

And this really was a crowd. She'd never seen anything quite like it at an art exhibition. A rock concert, yes. A crowded platform at a train station during rush hour when the trains were delayed, yes. But an exhibition of seventy-year-old paintings by an artist nobody had ever heard of?

It had to be news of the discovery of the tunnel beneath the grounds of the university, coupled with the mystery of the break in at the fortress. Gagliardi and his paintings were gathering a puzzling mystery around themselves, and bringing out all the amateur detectives in the local area.

'Stay close to me,' Jessica said to Caterina and Tomasso.

Caterina took hold of her brother's hand, much to his displeasure. The young boy looked bored already, and Jessica was regretting allowing them to come with her. An exhibition of paintings was obviously nowhere near as exciting as Tomasso had believed them to be, and it didn't look like Caterina was going to have an opportunity to sketch more drawings of Gagliardi's portraits.

After a few minutes of being jostled

and pushed, Jessica managed to get to stand in front of one of the paintings, Caterina and Tomasso by her side. Now that she could see the portrait up close, she was even more certain that this was Julian the Hospitaller depicted in the painting. It was a good job she didn't have a marker pen on her, as the temptation to reach out and draw a moustache on his face and put a sword in his hand might have been too strong to resist.

'It is him, isn't it?' Caterina said.

'Definitely,' Jessica replied.

'Are you going to tell anyone?'

'You know, I hadn't thought of that,' Jessica said. 'No one knows but us, do they?'

'Knows what, my dear?'

Jessica jumped, startled by the voice at her side. She turned to see William, leaning on his walking stick, gazing up at the painting on the wall.

He looked at Jessica and smiled. 'I'm sorry, I didn't mean to startle you.'

'Oh, that's all right,' Jessica said.

'And who are your two young companions?' he said, and smiled.

'This is Caterina and Tomasso, the children of the couple I'm staying with while I'm here,' Jessica replied.

'How delightful,' William said, and looked around. 'My, it really is very busy today, isn't it?'

'Yes, it's too busy,' Jessica said. 'Will you be all right in all these crowds?'

William chuckled. 'Oh don't worry about me.' He raised his walking stick. 'If anybody gets too close, I can always prod them with this!'

'Jessica?' Caterina said. 'Tomasso wants to go to the toilet.'

A sudden feeling of unease washed over Jessica. She had planned to not let the children out of her sight while they were in the city, but she hadn't considered the fact that she couldn't follow Tomasso into the men's toilets. She glanced around the crowded gallery, looking for Cora and Willem. She hadn't seen them all morning, but she couldn't shake the feeling that they might be somewhere very near.

'My dear, are you all right?' the old man said. 'You look troubled.'

'No, no, I'm fine,' Jessica said, feeling anything but. 'Actually, it's this crowd. I hate crowds.' She turned to the children. 'Let's find you a toilet and then we'll go, shall we?'

'Well, it was nice to meet you again, even if only briefly,' William said.

'Yes, you too,' Jessica said, distracted as Caterina and Tomasso began threading their way through the mass of bodies towards the toilets.

She began following them, but had only taken a few steps before she was aware of a commotion behind her. Turning to look, she saw that William appeared to be in the middle of a faint. The old man had been fortunate to have so many people around him, as he was being slowly lowered to the ground by a man and a woman who had caught him. More people moved toward him, concerned for his wellbeing. Jessica moved with them. What had happened?

The stifling closeness of the crowded gallery must have been too much for him after all.

Jessica stopped and was jostled as others pushed past her. It was her natural inclination to be concerned, to go and help, but she didn't need to. There were lots of people here, and she had Caterina and Tomasso to think about.

Jessica turned her back on the old man and began pushing her way against the flow of people, all of them attracted by the commotion and eager to find out more. Panic began to bite at the edges of Jessica's nerves. She had lost sight of the two children.

Calm down, they're fine, she told herself. *This is just the events of the last few days, making you worry too much.*

And then she caught sight of Caterina in a corridor outside of the gallery, beneath a sign that said *WC Maschile.* Jessica joined her and sighed with relief.

'I lost you for a moment or two,' she

said to the young girl.

'Tomasso was desperate for a wee,' Caterina said, grinning.

'Oh, I know that feeling! You know what? I've had enough of this place. Shall we go and grab something to eat now?'

'Can we ask Noah if he wants to come with us?' Caterina asked.

'Sure, that would be great!'

Caterina smiled self-consciously. 'Tomasso, he told me he saw you and Noah kissing.'

Jessica blushed. *Why do I keep doing that?*

'I think it's great,' Caterina said. 'I like Noah.'

'Good. I like him too,' Jessica said, and smiled.

'Do you think he was serious when he said I am good at drawing?'

'Absolutely, totally and one hundred percent serious,' Jessica said. 'Caterina, you're an amazingly talented artist. Is that something you'd like to pursue as a career when you finish school?'

Caterina nodded enthusiastically. 'Oh yes, I'd love to.'

Jessica glanced at the toilet door. 'Does Tomasso usually take this long in the toilets?'

'No, he's usually in and out really quick.'

That feeling of unease and mild panic began to creep up Jessica's chest once more. The last time she had seen Tomasso had been when she was talking to William, when Caterina told her that he needed the toilet. She hadn't seen him enter the toilets. But Caterina had. Hadn't she?

'Caterina,' Jessica said, 'you did see Tomasso come into these toilets, didn't you?'

Caterina turned white, and her eyes grew round and wide. 'No, he ran off ahead of me, he was so desperate. But he was headed here, he had to be. I was only a second behind him, I know I was!'

Jessica rapped her knuckles on the

door to the toilets. 'Tomasso!' she shouted.

Nothing.

Jessica opened the door and looked inside. It was only a small room, with two urinals and two cubicles. Jessica stepped inside. She pushed open the first cubicle door, and it swung back easily and silently.

The cubicle was empty.

The second cubicle was locked, the red 'engaged' sign showing. The Italian was *impegnato*. Jessica heard movement inside.

'Tomasso?' she said.

'*Per favore lasciami in pace, sto andando al gabinetto!*' a deep, gruff male voice said.

Jessica spun round, her eyes darting wildly around the washroom. There was nowhere else for Tomasso to be.

He was missing.

15

As night drew in, Jessica sat with Stefania and Fabrizio in their living room, waiting by the telephone. Angela sat with them, and was uncharacteristically quiet for once. Caterina, exhausted from worry, had gone to bed.

Noah entered the living room carrying a tray laden down with coffees and teas. 'Here we are,' he said, placing the cups on the coffee table. He sat down too.

Nobody said anything.

Jessica finally stirred, her limbs moving so slowly they felt like they were stuck in treacle. 'I am so, so sorry,' she said for what seemed like the thousandth time. 'I should never have taken Tomasso and Caterina out with me. I shouldn't have let them out of my sight.'

Stefania laid a hand on Jessica's and said, 'Shush, now. It is not your fault. The *polizia* will find him, I know they will.'

But her voice trembled as she spoke, and Jessica could see she was close to tears. 'I just don't understand where he went, or how he could have disappeared so quickly,' Jessica said, close to tears herself.

'The *polizia* will find him!' Fabrizio said forcefully. 'They must!'

'What about that awful woman you told us about?' Angela said. 'Could she have anything to do with this?'

Noah shifted on the sofa. 'I already told the police all about Cora and Willem. They don't see a connection, but they said they'd investigate.'

Jessica covered her face with her hands and massaged her forehead. A headache was brewing deep inside her skull. Her stomach was knotted up and churning with worry.

'Cora might have gone off the rails — she's obviously in with some unpleasant people and organisations now — but I can't see her kidnapping a child,' Noah said.

No one replied to his comment. The room seemed deafening to Jessica in its silence. Concern for Tomasso's safety, and guilt at having lost him when he had been in her care, twisted like snakes through her insides. *How could I have been so stupid?*

The silence of the room was broken by the shrill ring of a telephone. Stefania grabbed it and said, '*Pronto?*'

But the telephone rang again. Stefania held the phone away and looked at it, her forehead creased up in worry and puzzlement.

'It's mine,' Noah said, picking up his mobile from the table. 'Hello?' he said. His face clouded over as he listened to the speaker. Finally he disconnected without a word and placed the mobile gently back on the coffee table, almost as though it was a bomb and he didn't want to set it off.

'You were right after all,' he said to Angela, his voice low and deep. 'That was Cora. She says that she and Willem have Tomasso.'

Stefania cried out as though she was in physical pain.

Fabrizio stood up. 'Then we must call the *polizia* and tell them.'

Noah shook his head. Jessica had never seen him look so serious and worried. With his hair cut and his beard shaved off, he looked even more handsome than she had imagined he might. But now wasn't the time to be thinking about things like that. Jessica felt guilty even that the thought had entered her head.

'Cora said we'd never see Tomasso again if we called the police,' Noah said. 'And I think I believe her.'

'But what do they want with my boy?' Stefania wailed.

Noah looked up. 'It's not Tomasso they want. It's Jessica.'

Jessica's face turned cold at the mention of her name. 'Me? But what do they want with me?'

'The key to the trapdoor in my office,' Noah said. 'They seem to think you have it.'

'But I don't ... ' Jessica remembered, then, slipping the key into her pocket for safekeeping after she had climbed out of the tunnel.

She stood up and ran into her bedroom, rifling through her clothes until she found the key. She held it up in front of her face like a talisman.

'We need to take it to them,' Noah said, standing in the doorway.

Stefania and Fabrizio were crowded behind him. 'I am coming with you,' Fabrizio said.

'Of course,' Noah replied.

'Where are they?' Jessica said.

'Where do you think?' Noah said. 'Cora called me from my office at the university.'

'Then what are we waiting for?' Jessica said. 'Let's go.'

* * *

The university was in darkness when they arrived. Jessica had never seen the buildings and the grounds so quiet and empty of people. The university didn't seem the same somehow. During the day it was an attractive, pleasant place to be, full of life and happiness. But now, silent and dark, it exuded menace.

Maybe that was because Jessica and Noah were here to meet two kidnappers, to exchange a key for a child. To deal with the devil, it seemed to Jessica.

'There are no lights on in your office,' Jessica whispered as they approached the main campus building. 'Are you sure they're here?'

'They're here,' Noah said grimly.

The main entrance was open already. He had a torch, which he flicked on and used to guide them through the darkened corridors. Their footsteps echoed through the halls — another eerie element to add to the darkness and the silence, and unsettling Jessica even more.

Cora was waiting for them outside

Noah's office in a figure hugging T-shirt and jeans. Black, of course. Jessica saw the tip of the swastika tattoo on her arm, visible beneath the edge of the T-shirt sleeve.

'You're late,' she said. 'We have — '

'Where's Tomasso?' Jessica snapped, interrupting her.

The woman smiled languidly. Jessica fought hard to control the shiver the smile sent through her.

'Did you bring the key?' Cora said.

'Of course we did,' Noah said. 'Now, where's Tomasso?'

'He's inside, with Willem,' Cora replied, indicating Noah's closed door. 'And . . . '

'And what?' Noah said.

Cora smirked. 'You'll see.'

Jessica and Noah exchanged glances. Jessica's stomach churned with unease.

Cora opened the office door. The inside was lit from the beams of a couple of torches. Jessica wondered why they hadn't seen the light from outside. They all stepped through the doorway, into the darkened office.

Tomasso was huddled in a corner, his hands and feet bound together with wide strips of builder's tape. His mouth was covered with a gag. He looked at Jessica and Noah with big round eyes, wet with tears.

'No!' Jessica gasped. 'How could you?'

Willem stepped from the shadows like a ghost appearing from the dark. 'It was simple,' he said. 'You were distracted so easily, we were able to snatch the boy in the toilets and whisk him away before you even noticed he'd gone.'

Jessica remembered the old man, William, having some sort of fainting episode; remembered the crowd in the gallery closing in on him as people tried to help.

'You took advantage of that poor old man as he fainted,' Jessica gasped. 'You must have been following us, waiting for your opportunity.'

A heavily accented voice spoke from

a darkened corner of the room. 'No, we do not wait for opportunities, Jessica Matthews. We create them.'

The voice, although she was sure she had never heard it before, still sounded vaguely familiar. Jessica was aware of a figure sitting in a chair, but the light from the torches did nothing to illuminate the corner in which he sat.

Cora leaned over Noah's desk and switched on his lamp.

'Hello, Jessica.'

Jessica gasped and clutched Noah's arm. 'William! What are you doing here?'

The old man smiled. 'My name is not William. I am Legend. Legend Niedermeyer.'

The darkened office suddenly seemed to close in on Jessica, trapping her. None of this could be happening, surely. It had to be a bad dream, a nightmare. The old man had always looked so friendly, and yet now here he was, and his appearance had altered somehow.

Now he looked evil.

'You can't be Legend Niedermeyer,' Noah said. 'If you'd even survived this long, you'd be in your nineties at the very least.'

'I was born in nineteen twenty-two,' Legend said, gripping the sides of his chair and slowly standing up. 'But as you can see, I am in perfect health for a man of my age.'

And Jessica could see it was true. Although he looked old, he appeared to be fit and healthy and strong. She noticed he wasn't holding his walking stick; that it was propped against the side of the chair. She had been right all along. It was obviously an affectation, perhaps to make him appear a little frailer than he was.

'Legend is our great-grandfather,' Cora said, gently placing a hand on his arm. 'And he's been teaching me and Willem in the ways of the old ones.'

'What nonsense are you talking now, Cora?' Noah said. 'You always were a fruitcake, but now you've gone completely over the edge.'

Don't antagonise them! Jessica thought.

Legend chuckled and took Cora's hand, and Willem's too. 'The Nazi party once had a vision to spread its wings over the entire world, to populate it with superhumans, with übermenschen! And now, that day is at hand once more!'

Jessica caught Noah glancing at her. For all his bravado, she could see he was scared. And she didn't blame him. She was terrified.

'And what has all that got to do with Lorenzo Gagliardi's paintings, and with the tunnel beneath the university?' Noah said.

'Don't you see it? Even now, are you blind to what's going on?' Cora said. 'We have no interest in Gagliardi or his ridiculous paintings. When we broke into the museum that night, we were simply looking for clues in his paintings.'

'Clues for what?' Noah said.

Legend raised Cora's and Willem's hands in the air, as though he was a referee at a boxing match and inexplicably pronouncing both fighters the winner. 'The sword! The sword of Julian!'

'Are you crazy?' Jessica gasped. She couldn't help it; the whole situation seemed so ridiculous.

'Julian's sword tasted the blood of the Devil,' said William, 'and was imbued with power — a power that can subdue the world. That's why the monks guarded it with their lives. They knew of its power; they knew what it was capable of, and they were scared.'

'And you believe the sword's here, beneath the university grounds,' Jessica said quietly.

'I don't just believe it, I know it is,' Niedermeyer said. 'And once I have it in my hands, once it has tasted blood once more, its dark power shall be mine!'

'You know, that's all fine and dandy, and I don't really give two flying hoots what's down there — could be the Ark of the Covenant for all I care.' Noah pointed at Tomasso, sitting silently in the corner. 'Right now, though, we're taking that little boy home.'

'The key,' Cora said.

Jessica slipped her hand in her pocket, her fingers closing around the key. She pulled it out and held out her hand.

The key to the trapdoor had always had a mysterious significance before now. It had always seemed important. But now it was simply a playing piece in a game that Jessica had never agreed to get involved in, and whose rules seemed to be changing as it progressed.

Cora took the key from her, their fingers touching briefly. Everyone watched in silence as Cora inserted the key into the trapdoor lock and tried turning it. She looked up at Noah and Jessica, her eyes blazing with fury. 'It's the wrong key!'

'You're holding it the wrong way round,' Jessica said, unable to disguise the smugness she felt. 'Place the handle in the lock and turn it clockwise.'

'Ingenious,' Niedermeyer whispered.

Cora held Jessica's gaze for a moment, obviously angry at having been tricked like this. Finally she turned back to the trapdoor and inserted the handle of the key into the lock. The tumblers fell into place as she turned the key.

Taking a firm grip of the round handle, Cora lifted the trapdoor. Rather than the excitement she had initially felt at the opening of the door into the underground passage, it seemed to Jessica this time that death was snaking its way into Noah's office from the bowels of the earth. She suppressed a shudder as she thought of the skeleton guarding the next locked door.

'Now, you've got what you wanted,' Noah said. 'Give us Tomasso and we will be on our way.'

'I'm afraid not,' Niedermeyer said. 'I think we will hold onto him a little longer, to ensure your continued cooperation.'

Jessica noticed Noah clenching his fist by his side as he visibly restrained himself from attacking the old man. For a second she was reminded of Gagliardi's portraits of Julian, and an idea stirred in the back of her mind.

'Who do you want to take with us?' Cora said. 'The child, or Jessica?'

Jessica's stomach turned over. What did she mean? What was she talking about?

Niedermeyer's gaze fell on Jessica first, and then Tomasso. The little boy looked up at him, wide-eyed. As if obeying a silent command, Willem strode across the office and took hold of Tomasso by the scruff of his T-shirt.

'No!' Niedermeyer commanded. 'I've changed my mind. We shall take the lovely Jessica with us.'

'What are you talking about?' Noah yelled. 'Take Jessica where?'

Niedermeyer smiled. 'The sword of Julian needs a sacrifice.'

'You crazy son of a — '

Willem stepped in front of the old man as Noah lunged for him, and shoved Noah in the chest. Noah staggered back into his desk, but managed to stay on his feet.

It was then that Jessica noticed the second statuette of Julian sitting on top of Noah's desk. He must have brought it up from the crypt. What had he been planning to do? Smash it open and get the second key from inside?

Jessica's thoughts were interrupted as she heard Willem growling and baring his teeth at Noah, like an animal ready to strike.

'Jessica shall be our sacrifice,' Niedermeyer said.

Cora pointed at Jessica. 'You, go first.'

Jessica looked at Cora, her mind a blank.

'Down into the tunnel! Now!' Cora hissed. 'And then I'll follow you.'

'You're wasting your time,' Noah said, speaking quickly. 'There's another door down there, and it's locked. And guess what? Nobody has the key.'

Jessica had to resist the urge to glance at the statuette of Julian. The fact that the second door was still locked was their only hope right now. If they were to find that second key, it was all over.

'Don't worry yourself about that, Mr Glassman,' Niedermeyer said.

Cora grabbed Jessica by her shirt and dragged her to the hole in the floor. 'You go first and I'll follow,' she hissed.

'Cora, this is madness!' Noah said. 'Surely you can see that? Please, think about what you're doing. This wasn't how you used to be, this isn't you.'

Cora smirked at him and pushed Jessica a little closer to the edge of the opening in the floor.

'Okay! Okay!' Jessica cried out. She turned to face Noah. 'It'll be all right. Don't worry, just look after Tomasso.'

Noah nodded stiffly, his face tight with tension.

Jessica sat down on the lip of the

trapdoor opening, her legs dangling into space. She was trembling. The last time she had climbed down here she had been wearing a harness. Now she had to make the descent without any safety gear, and her legs felt as weak as a newborn kitten's.

'Get moving,' Cora snapped.

Jessica twisted around onto her front and her feet found purchase in two of the holes in the stone wall. She took the steps carefully, lowering herself down.

When she had lowered herself enough that her chin was level with the floor, she paused and looked up at Noah. 'I love you,' she said.

'I love you, too,' Noah replied.

And with that, Jessica lowered herself into the darkness.

16

Jessica's hands were slick with sweat, and her arms and legs kept trembling. All of this made the climb more difficult than it had been the last time she had descended into the underworld beneath Noah's office. She moved slowly, carefully, with Cora following along close above, and blocking out the little light that was coming from the table lamp on Noah's desk.

Cora had a torch though, strapped to her head. Although it was seldom pointed Jessica's way, at least there was some light in the stone shaft, enough to pick out the handholds right in front of her face.

Jessica concentrated on keeping her breathing regular, trying to slow down her rapid heartbeat. She had to stay calm, alert for any opportunity to escape, or turn the tables on Cora.

As she descended deeper into the stone shaft, she heard movement and voices above. It took her a moment or two to realise what was going on. The old man, Legend Niedermeyer, was coming down too! Cora was giving him words of encouragement, and helping him place his feet in the gaps in the stonework. Jessica could hear Willem too, obviously doing his bit to help his great-grandfather climb down the hole.

Was this a chance for Noah? Could he use this distraction to disable Willem in some way? Jessica paused, unconsciously holding her breath, waiting.

'Get a move on!' Cora hissed above her. 'What are you waiting for?'

Jessica started her descent again. Perhaps Willem had tied Noah up, like they'd done with poor Tomasso.

When her feet finally touched the bottom, Jessica was in almost complete darkness. She had to kneel down on the muddy ground and use her hands to feel for the tunnel entrance in the side of the stone shaft. There wasn't room for three of them down here, so Jessica had to get inside the mouth of the tunnel opening as soon as she could.

She quickly found the gap. Lowering her head, scared of hitting it on the stone, she crawled into the dark space. After shuffling along in the pitch dark for a few moments, she paused when her way was lit from behind by a bright light. The torch beam cast a long shadow out in front of her.

'Does this lead to the locked chamber?' Cora said.

'Yes,' Jessica mumbled, unable to turn and look at Cora in the tight space.

'Then get moving. We must be quick.'

Jessica began shuffling forward again, and Cora followed. This time at least there was some illumination from Cora's head torch.

Jessica kept her head down, strands of her hair falling over her face and beads of sweat popping out on her forehead. What would Cora and Niedermeyer do when they got to the locked door and realised they couldn't get inside? Jessica was completely at their mercy down here. Would they take out their fury on her? She shook her head, trying not to think about this. *Just one step at a time*, she told herself.

The palms of her hands began to sting as she crawled on, and her knees grew sore. How far away were they from the door and the skeleton? The tunnel opened out there, at its end. There would be enough room for them all to gather together.

'How much further?' Cora hissed.

Jessica stopped crawling and took a deep, shaky breath. 'I'm not sure. Almost there, I think.'

'Then get moving,' the old man said, his voice strong and loud in the tunnel.

Jessica started crawling again, drawing closer to the locked chamber and the skeleton guarding it.

★   ★   ★

Noah kept clenching and unclenching his fists. He couldn't help it.

Willem watched him with a look of mild amusement on his face. They were facing each other across the office, Willem by the door, Noah standing by Tomasso. The little boy was still tied up and gagged.

'Can't we untie Tomasso?' Noah said.

Willem shook his head.

'You might act all tough, but the truth is, you're scared of a little boy, aren't you?'

Willem stared at Noah and said nothing. His arms were folded across his chest, and he leaned against the wall by the office door.

Noah sighed. 'You're a barrel of laughs. I bet you get invited to all the best parties.'

What are you trying to do, antagonise him? Noah thought. *I'm pretty sure that only works in the movies.*

Noah wondered how Jessica was, and if they had reached the locked underground chamber yet. His insides were tight with fear at the thought of what they had planned down there. What were they talking about, that the sword of Julian needed a sacrifice? Did they intend to use the sword on Jessica? Noah closed his eyes, pushing that thought away.

A sudden commotion, the sound of the door opening, Willem moving, had Noah snapping his eyes open again. Fabrizio had entered the room. His eyes widened as he saw Tomasso, bound and gagged. With all his attention fixed on his son, Fabrizio didn't notice Willem lunging for him.

'Fabrizio, look out!' Noah shouted.

Too late, Willem smashed into Fabrizio in a rugby tackle and the two men hit the floor hard. Noah ran to help, but Willem was already on his feet, his teeth bared like a snarling dog. From a pocket he produced a black knuckle duster and slipped it over his fingers, clenching it in his fist.

Oh no, Noah thought. *He'll rip us apart with that thing.*

Suddenly he noticed Fabrizio climbing quietly to his feet behind Willem.

'Aww, come on pretty boy,' Noah said to Willem, keeping him distracted. 'Let's play nice, shall we?'

Willem's snarl turned into a twisted smile, and Noah wasn't sure which one looked more frightening.

The smile slipped, and Willem's eyes widened as he heard movement from behind. He turned, but too late as Fabrizio picked up the statuette of Julian from Noah's desk and slammed it onto the back of Willem's head. Willem's eyes rolled back, and then he crumpled to the floor.

'Tomasso!' Fabrizio cried, and rushed to his son, enveloping him in a huge hug.

Noah checked on Willem whilst Fabrizio untied Tomasso.

'Is he dead?' Fabrizio asked.

'No. He's out cold, but he's alive.'

Fabrizio pulled the gag off Tomasso's mouth. 'Good. Despite what he has done, I could not bear the thought that I had killed a man.'

Tomasso and Fabrizio hugged each

other, the little boy talking in Italian to his father, the words tumbling over one another.

Willem lay amongst the shards of Julian's statuette, which had smashed when Fabrizio had dropped it after slamming it on Willem's skull.

The key! Noah thought.

He ran his fingers through the shards of pottery.

Nothing.

He turned to face the square hole in the floor of his office, thinking about Jessica, and about the locked door down there. Thinking about Cora and Legend, and what they might do.

I have to get down there, Noah thought. *I can't let them hurt Jessica!*

★ ★ ★

They were all gathered outside the heavy wooden door, the skeleton lying in front of it, when they heard yells from up in Noah's office, and the sound of something smashing.

'We must work quickly,' Legend Niedermeyer said, looking at Cora. 'Willem has obviously been overpowered, and no doubt the police will be on their way.'

Cora pulled the key from her pocket and inserted its handle into the door and tried turning it counter-clockwise.

Nothing. The key would not move. She uttered an oath of frustration and anger.

'Quickly, quickly!' Niedermeyer said.

Cora withdrew the key and turned it around, inserting it the proper way into the lock. This time the key did turn, and the tumblers fell into place.

Jessica mentally kicked herself. The same key had opened both doors. Why hadn't they thought of that?

Cora pulled at the door.

Nothing.

She gave it a shove and this time it moved, gave way before the palm of her hand. A cool breeze washed over them, but the air was stale.

Niedermeyer crawled through the

open doorway first, his head torch illuminating the way before him. Cora indicated that Jessica should go next.

'Jessica!' Noah's voice echoed down the stone shaft to her.

'I'm here!' Jessica called, just before Cora slapped her hand tight over Jessica's mouth and silenced her.

Cora roughly shoved her through the square doorway. She scuffed herself on the dirty, rocky ground as Cora followed.

Looking up from the ground, catching her breath, Jessica could see that they were in a large chamber hewn out of the rock. Legend and Cora silently played their torch lights over the walls and the ceiling and across the ground.

Sacks of gold filled the opposite half of the chamber, glinting yellow in the light of the torch beams. Jessica could hardly believe her eyes. The legend was true. This had to be what was left of Julian's gold, given to the monks of the abbey upon his death.

And there, on a stone altar in front of

the sacks of gold, lay a sword. The sword of Julian.

'Yes!' hissed Niedermeyer. 'The sword — it's mine!'

Cora grabbed hold of Jessica, pulling her further into the chamber.

Niedermeyer stood over the sword and reached out, his hand trembling. His fingers closed around the hilt. He lifted it from the stone altar.

The sword was obviously heavy and ungainly and he struggled to hold it upright, having to use both hands.

'Bring her to the altar!' Niedermeyer shouted.

Jessica struggled against Cora, but the woman's grip was too firm. Cora started pulling her to the miniature stone altar, dragging her along the rocky ground.

'No!'

It was Noah, clambering through the open hatch into the chamber. Jessica took advantage of the surprise by struggling against Cora and managing to pull an arm free.

Legend Niedermeyer let out a terrible high-pitched shriek and lifted the sword over his head. Jessica could see he was no longer prepared to wait for her to be dragged over to the altar, and that he was ready to bring the sword down on her right now.

The sword of Julian needs a sacrifice, she thought as everyone stood frozen, unable to act, it seemed, until Legend had brought the sword down in its killing arc.

Legend let the sword fall in a graceful curve, straight for Jessica.

* * *

Fabrizio held Tomasso close, staring uneasily at the open trapdoor. He could hear shouts from down below. What was happening? Should he go down and help Noah?

Fabrizio glanced at Willem, still lying unconscious on the floor. No, his place was with Tomasso. And besides, he could hear the *polizia*, their sirens blaring as they pulled into the university grounds. They would be here any moment now, and they would take over. He just hoped they weren't too late, and that Jessica would be all right.

Another shout echoed up from the stone shaft, and Tomasso began struggling in his father's arms and wrenched himself free.

'Tomasso, no!' Fabrizio shouted as his boy ran to the opening in the office floor.

Tomasso stopped at the square hatch and leaned over it. And taking a deep breath, he shouted, 'Hey you! You wanna fight?'

* * *

Tomasso's war cry echoed down through the tunnel and into the chamber, startling Legend Niedermeyer as he wielded the sword of Julian, the ancient weapon slicing down towards Jessica. The sword's arc was deflected, as though some invisible force had knocked it off its path. The blade hit the rocky ground with a loud clang, and shattered into several pieces.

Legend cried out in pain as the shock of the impact travelled up through his arms and sent him reeling to the ground.

Cora turned to help her great-grandfather, and Jessica pulled her other arm free and gave Cora a good shove in the back, sending her sprawling. Before she could get back on her feet, Noah was standing over her.

'Stay right where you are,' he said. 'The police are on their way down here now. It's over, Cora.'

Already Jessica could hear movement echoing through the tunnel, and men shouting out in Italian.

'It is really all over now, isn't it?' Jessica said.

Noah nodded, smiling. 'It sure is. You're safe now.'

Jessica fell into Noah's arms and gripped him tight.

17

'Are you serious?' Jessica said.

'Absolutely,' Noah replied.

'Well, I think it's a load of stuff and nonsense,' Angela said. 'You're all cracked, I know you are.'

'I believe you,' Caterina said.

'Well, I'm glad somebody does,' Noah laughed. 'Thank you, Caterina.'

They were sitting outside, the late evening sun comfortably warm, drinking wine and discussing the events of the last few days. Stefania and Fabrizio were there, with Tomasso, his head lowered as he studiously played on a handheld computer game.

'But what makes you so sure?' Caterina said.

'Well, let's look at the evidence,' Noah said. 'First of all, Lorenzo Gagliardi was supposed to have given his life over to guarding the sword of

Julian at the abbey. But then he left the abbey to pursue his passion for painting. Then the war broke out and northern Italy was occupied by the Germans. Suddenly, Gagliardi was a prisoner of war. Why?'

'Because he was a spy?' Caterina said.

Noah laughed. 'No, not quite. Because Legend Niedermeyer believed that the sword of Julian held supernatural powers and that if he could find it he could harness those powers for Hitler to conquer the world. And he must have been aware that the monks at the abbey held the secret to its whereabouts.'

'But why did he imprison Gagliardi?' Jessica asked. 'Why not one of the monks from the abbey?'

'Because the abbey had been bombed earlier in the war, killing all the monks inside. Gagliardi was the last one left.'

'That explains all the visits to the fortress by Legend during Gagliardi's imprisonment,' Jessica said.

'Exactly. And then the allies won the

war, Gagliardi was released, and Legend went into hiding.'

'But what about all the portraits of Julian that Gagliardi painted after his release?' Caterina asked.

'This is where I am getting to the point of my argument,' Noah said. 'I believe that while he was in prison, the spirit of Julian the Hospitaller protected him from Nazi questioning. Gagliardi was a mild-mannered artist and former monk. How else could he have withstood the torture he must have gone through? And then, when he was released, he couldn't get Julian out of his head, was obsessed by him, and had to paint his portrait over and over again.'

'And you're saying Julian's ghost protected me, in that cavern?' Jessica said. 'That his spirit knocked the sword to one side as Legend brought it down?'

'Yes, I am,' Noah said.

Silence greeted that last remark. Finally Jessica shook her head. 'But I don't believe in ghosts.'

'Neither do I,' Noah said. 'But it's the only explanation I've got.'

Everybody sat in silence, thinking this over.

'Well I believe you,' Caterina said again. 'And I believe in ghosts, too.'

'But why did Cora and Willem slice open that painting in the fortress?' Jessica asked, looking at Noah.

Noah shrugged. 'I think they were probably looking for clues. They probably thought that Gagliardi had left signs within the paintings somehow indicating where the sword might be.'

'They're all mad if you ask me,' Angela said.

'And that's why they stole Caterina's drawing too,' Noah said. 'They thought she had stumbled onto something, they just didn't know what.'

Jessica shook her head. 'I thought I was on a studious break in Italy studying paintings and history. If I'd known what I was letting myself in for . . .'

'Yes, it's been an exciting few days,

hasn't it?' Stefania said with a smile. 'But at least something wonderful came out of it.'

'What's that, then?' Noah asked.

'Why, you and Jessica, of course!' Stefania cried out. 'I could see the two of you were meant for each other from the first moment I saw you together.'

'Really?' Jessica said, taking Noah's hand and giving it a squeeze.

'As plain as the nose on your face, it was,' Angela said. 'The two of you were completely besotted with each other.'

'And then Tomasso saw you kissing,' Caterina said, and giggled.

Tomasso looked up from his game at hearing his name mentioned. 'Hey you!' he said.

'You wanna fight?' everyone shouted back at him in unison, and then burst out laughing.

Jessica looked at Noah, who was already gazing at her, a soft smile on his face.

'I love you,' she whispered.

'I love you too,' he whispered back.

Jessica Matthews might not have come to Italy looking for romance, but romance had found her.

And she didn't mind one bit.

WHAT HAPPENS IN NASHVILLE

Angela Britnell

Claire Buchan is hardly over the moon about travelling to Nashville, Tennessee for her sister's hen party: a week of honky-tonks, karaoke and cowboys. Certainly not strait-laced Claire's idea of a good time, what with her lawyer job and sensible boyfriend, Philip. But then she doesn't bank on meeting Rafe Cavanna. On the surface, Rafe fits the cowboy stereotype, with his handsome looks and roguish charm. But as he and Claire get to know each other, she realises there is far more to him than meets the eye . . .

GRAND DESIGNS

Linda Mitchelmore

Interior decorator Carrie Fraser cannot believe her luck when she is invited to work at beautiful Oakenbury Hall. Nor can she quite get over the owner of the Hall, the gorgeous and wealthy Morgan Harrington. Morgan is bound by his late father's wishes to keep Oakenbury within the family and have children; and the more time Carrie spends with him, the more she yearns to be the woman to fulfil this wish. But the likes of Carrie Fraser could never be enough for a high-flying businessman like Morgan . . . could she?